A Suit To South Korea

By
K.G. Munro

MAPLE
PUBLISHERS

A Suitcase To South Korea

Author: K.G. Munro

Copyright © K.G. Munro (2024)

The right of K.G. Munro to be identified as author of this work has been asserted by the author in accordance with section 77 and 78 of the Copyright, Designs and Patents Act 1988.

First Published in 2024

ISBN 978-1-83538-310-0 (Paperback)
      978-1-83538-311-7 (E-Book)

Book layout by:
    White Magic Studios
    www.whitemagicstudios.co.uk

Published by:
    Maple Publishers
    Fairbourne Drive, Atterbury,
    Milton Keynes,
    MK10 9RG, UK
    www.maplepublishers.com

A CIP catalogue record for this title is available from the British Library.

CONTENTS

Chapter One

A Mistake In A Deadline Destiny

Material objects that are most treasured always find a way to go awry at the worst of times, as Autumn Willows' discovered whilst she stood at the airport, with the wrong suitcase.

Precious time passed her by as Autumn, a 28-year old Canadian author from Alberta, glanced upon the leathery tanned brown suitcase slumped on the ground, in utter despair. Her heart clawed insistently at her throat, there were no words to convey the desperation she felt looking around the airport trying to find her suitcase that held within its sacred confines her beloved manuscript. The faces of strangers went by in a blur, her Korean was limited so she couldn't ask the questions she needed, nor could she understand the answers even if she received them. She briskly walked around the airport; her suitcase was black, medium-sized with a metallic handle that had her zodiac sign engraved on it. Sweat quivered on her straight plucked russet brows as she pushed past crowds of people until she found a free spot to rest. She puffed and panted, letting go of the suitcase for a minute as she tried to regain herself.

"I wish today was over already," she grumbled flexing her tired hand.

Howbeit, her respite became short-lived when the ground beneath her feet started to quake, and shrill screams came from the entryway of the airport. She instantly froze clutching onto the suitcase as a horde of boisterous young people came stampeding in her direction. She blinked before drowning in a sea of fans and their rainbow of handmade fan signs.

Meanwhile, a group of young men were retrieving their luggage as a gaggle of screaming fans approached them. The oldest member who was 29 years old, Taeyang Chan, rolled his eyes yanking on his stubborn suitcase that had been refusing to budge from the conveyer belt. The flight from Taiwan to South Korea had been crammed, noisy, humid, and overbearing. All he wanted to do from this point onward was wolf down a ham and jalapeno pizza then take a nap in peace. On days like this, being a part of Dark Star Seven – one of the biggest K-pop groups in Korea – was a major hassle. One which they all dealt with differently. Hyeon, the group's youngest member at 21 years old, accidentally bumped into his side. He gave him a glare but said nothing as he finally freed his suitcase.

Another member called Soon Woo, who is 24 and very outgoing, winked at the gaggling girls who were practically salivating at his presence and started signing autographs as they screamed and grabbed at his toned veiny arms. He lived for the attention, which only exacerbated the fans' crazy reactions. Taeyang rolled his eyes at this, they had just returned from promoting their new single and had a tight schedule so the last thing he needed was one of his boys playing Mr. Boyfriend for every passing lady. Soon Woo was one of the main vocalists in the group but the sexiest member who was known for being promiscuous and was a bit of an alleged gambler too. Kim Huang, at 27, is the second oldest member, and best dancer stroke qualified yoga instructor, he ignored them all as he went outside to the car first. Before heading off, Taeyang flicked Soon Woo's ear as he pushed past Ha Rin, 26, the group's secondary vocalist. Taemin Lee, 25, the group's visual, and Baekhyun Hasa, 23, the group's main rapper - they looked at each other and shrugged at their leader's grouchiness.

Each member made it outside with their luggage and were ushered into a decoy unmarked dark van with tinted windows as fans swarmed all around them like ravenous locusts. Adrenaline mixed with nervous tension fuelled each member as they repeated this ritual, which had become so familiar to them over the last couple of years. They drove around the corner and into another part of the airport as security kept the rather zealous crowds away. Once the word was given, the boys were ordered to leave the fake car and head straight to the real car that was going to take them back to their dorm.

Thanks to security, they made it safely to their real car, the boys piled in one by one followed by their manager, Chen, who sat at the front next to the driver. Taeyang sat on the right-hand side of the car with Soon Woo next to him. Now that the hordes of people were gone, he took the opportunity to dive into his suitcase to get his face mist and freshen up. Taeyang pulled his suitcase onto his lap licking his cracked lips. He did a double take at what he saw. He examined the suitcase, skepticism danced around his wide and rich hazel orbs. The first indication that something was amiss was the fact that his suitcase had magically turned from tanned brown, heavy, with rickety wheels to black, virtually brand new, and with a Pisces zodiac sign carved into the metallic handle. He huffed and placed the suitcase on its side, grabbing the small zip. Hyeon gave his leader a curious stare. Taeyang shrugged him off unzipping the suitcase before pausing, his face turning beet red at what he discovered.

Sitting in front of him were sets of clean white lace bras, and undergarments. His cheeks sizzled with a rosy apple hue as his throat clammed up at the sight. Hyeon pulled one of the fancy bras up, jiggling it playfully before Taeyang slapped it back into the suitcase giving the young man a severe glare. Soon Woo on the other hand gave his friend a knowing look and a quick wink. In response to this Taeyang punched Soon Woo's shoulder causing him to hiss which caught their manager's attention.

The boys froze as their manager gave them a serious glance whilst slightly lowering his round glasses. Taeyang smiled at Chen who returned the gesture with a puzzled look before resuming what looked to be a crossword game. Hyeon cast his gaze to the world passing by trying to hide his blushing face whilst Soon Woo pulled out peppermint gum from his pocket and busied himself with that. After a few minutes, Taeyang turned his attention back to the suitcase sifting across the lingerie. Underneath, the risqué clothing he found a manuscript. He gently pulled the thick document held together with twine out and closed over the suitcase. Hyeon looked back towards him with curiosity budding in the depths of his jade orbs. A name along with other details was stamped in ruby ink across the top right corner in English. He made a note of that. Taeyang pushed past the first page, each detail was done to precision. He was steeped in curiosity as he continued reading before turning another page. Smaller details like the paper quality really impressed him, she had used 100 gsm offset paper, each flick of the page was like a feathery wisp against his fatigued fingertips. Taeyang found himself enjoying the handiwork of this particular writer. A flurry of words skated across his eyes, inviting him into a world of turbulence, paradoxical safety, and adventure.

He thumbed the pages thoughtfully, ignoring his fellow bandmates who were messing around behind him. Whoever this Autumn Willows' was, it was obvious that she had put an enormous amount of effort into this manuscript. He wasn't familiar with the ins and outs of the writing world, but he did know that any project with this level of detail and passion emanating from the pages was a result of many sleepless nights of work, love, and determination. Taeyang could relate to those sacrifices; he spent most of his time training, when he wasn't doing variety shows, banal interviews, or working in the studio with the rest of the group. Taeyang considered his options, he knew her name, and e-mail since it was stamped onto the top of the document. So, he could e-mail her letting her know he had it. "What if she doesn't get it in time?" he thought to himself. Taeyang groaned, holding his head in his hands as the manuscript sat snugly on his lap.

Autumn sat in an independent café that was based in the heart of Seoul, she stirred her Americano watching the world go by. The café emanated a chill vibe since it was moderately empty except for another table where a random woman was typing away on a laptop. She left the airport a while ago after surviving a wave of insane fans she had sadly been caught up in with the tanned brown suitcase she had received fortunately still in hand. She hadn't dared open it. Aside from the act itself being an invasion of privacy, it was unclear who owned this beaten-up excuse for a suitcase. Back at the Airport, her panic, and rushing around had prevented her from getting a better look at the suitcase. Upon closer inspection she did notice more details. The plastic wheels were crooked and wallpapered with scratches. Based on that she could deduce that the owner must either be a frequent traveller or a complete cheapskate.

She sipped on her lukewarm coffee as an idea flashed into her head. "The tag! There must be a tag on it!" she thought to herself, setting down her cup onto the glass table before hoisting the suitcase onto her lap in a way that made certain that her floral dress didn't get dirtied. She moved it, looking to the chunky zip where she found a white plastic tag dangling around. Using her thumb and forefinger, she lifted it closer, the writing was small and in scribbly blue ink. Autumn only understood the number, and the name but it was better than nothing. She placed it back onto the floor, bumping the table slightly in the process causing a little bit of her coffee to spill. For the past couple of weeks, she had been on the last part of her book tour, she thought that after finishing up in Taiwan that would be her done. That she could hand her new manuscript into her publisher and call it a day for a while. But the flight ended up here as a layover, that's what it was supposed to be but it seemed that destiny had other ideas. "Not the greatest ones," she thought sullenly, looking at the table that now adorned a puddle of coffee. She used a crisp white napkin that had been provided with her order to clean up the mess. Autumn pulled out a few South Korean Won and left it on top of the bill. She tucked her vintage looking leather wallet back into the deep pocket of her dress. She dabbed her mouth clean with another napkin before taking the suitcase and leaving the establishment.

Stars gleamed above the crisp summer night as the daylight became an illusion replaced by galactic skies of black mixed with streaks of purple. Taeyang and Hyeon were walking down the streets of Seoul as they returned from an arduous session of dancing. One that their manager had so kindly sprung on them last minute. The two of them ended up being held back longer because the instructor was less than satisfied with their performance today. Taeyang yawned, the trek back to the dorm was a substantial one. His mind still mulling over the manuscript he now had in his possession but also what had become of his precious suitcase. There wasn't anything of intrinsic value in the luggage, but it was still his stuff. Lost in his own world, he was closely followed by Hyeon who kept yawning also as he dragged his throbbing feet. This particular practice had been brutal on Taeyang's ankle that was still in the process of healing after he had fallen off the stage whilst performing the week prior. He wobbled as he continued walking, flinching at the pain. They made small talk from time to time, but it was an unusual noise in the distance that made Taeyang stop in his tracks.

His ears twitched; a familiar brush of suspicion stroked the edge of his senses. He held out his sweaty arm to stop his counterpart who, albeit confused by his leader's actions, stopped walking. Taeyang slowly turned around, his heart thudding, an icy sweat dribbled down his back making him want to shiver. Behind them sat parked cars, and shadows of the buildings cast by the streetlights. In spite of the fact that no one appeared to be around, he still wasn't convinced. He is one of the top idols in South Korea, in fact, their group recently started promotions overseas to bolster their reputation abroad. Knowing this along with his less than pleasant past experiences, he knew a stalker when he sensed one. Taeyang put his finger to his lips and signalled Hyeon to proceed forward without hesitation.

Once, Hyeon was a good distance away, he investigated the area. Hyeon had experienced a particularly nasty ordeal with a crazy fan just a couple of months ago, so Taeyang wanted to protect him. He's the toughest in the group, with a black belt in judo, karate, and kickboxing experience so was confident that he could kick some ass if he needed to. A rustling noise brought him back to reality as he continued to look around. He shivered; the night's coolness started to permeate the formfitting cotton of his sweatshirt. Taeyang continued looking between each side of the road. A sense of discomfort still lingered as he ventured further from where he had come. Sweat dribbled down his still pinkish cheek, his hands clenched before unclenching. Another noise made him snap his head around; a stray tabby cat scurried away from a car that began flashing orange, and blaring as the alarm went off. He kicked a random used tin into the gutter before his shoulders relaxed. A close call, that's all it was, just paranoia and bad experiences toying in his head.

Taeyang turned away mere feet from the source of his disconcertment. It was getting late; the night was shifting into a bone seeping chill. He sighed, being an idol became tough when it came to situations like this, but that's a pain he had to and would continue to endure for this dream. One he had worked endlessly to achieve and had sacrificed a lot to be able to do. He started to head back in his original direction not noticing the shadows moving just out of eyeshot. Once the coast was clear, two girls peeked out from behind a building with smirks decorating their plotting faces. A camera firmly nestled within the shorter girl's stubby palm. She leaned further over the wall and held up the camera snapping a couple of additional photos before slinking back behind it into the shadows. The girls gave each other a single but resolute nod as they locked eyes. The duo then faded back into obscurity; their giggling drowned out as blaring police cars rushed down the road.

Autumn trudged the cold and rather lonely streets of Seoul. Her mind became hazy with fatigue and acute dehydration. Finding a payphone had been harder than she had originally anticipated and since her smartphone was in her luggage, that she didn't currently have, she had no other choice but to try and find one. Booking a place to stay was its own challenge since this place was meant to be a stopover not a full trip and most of the hotels were booked up with tourists. She wrapped her thin coat around her body, her feet started to swell, and throb, protesting against her ceaseless movements. Her morale plummeted with every passing narrow street she walked. In her drowsy state she failed to see a man advancing towards her causing her body to collide with his. The force of his body knocked her own onto the ground, her eyes watered before clenching shut at the sudden sharp pain that emanated from her tailbone, after a few seconds she shook it off. The tall stranger grumbled something under his breath before regaining his balance and walking off, not giving her the chance to say 'sorry' for bumping into him. Autumn picked herself up from the ground wincing whilst she stood at her full height. Checking her coat, she noticed a dark brown mark and a rip in the soft material, so she wiped it off the best that she could and decided to throw out the coat once daylight arrived. With that in mind she sussed out the rest of the area, taking note of the sketchy unlit alleyways before continuing down the road stepping in a freezing murky puddle in the process.

"Dammit!" she cursed before violently shaking off her foot and stamping away.

Taeyang was a stone's throw away from the dorm when it happened. A random woman crashed into him knocking off his balance. He managed to catch himself falling back with his hand before he completely fell to the ground, but he wasn't amused that on top of his ankle pain he now had to contend with his wrist hurting. When he looked at her, he saw that she had fallen onto her butt which caused him to glare.

"Stupid girl," he remarked before he stood up and walked off.

He didn't care to hear whatever feeble excuse she would use for being careless, he just wanted to go to bed and sleep for a change.

Autumn found a phone box after walking a bit farther, both of her heels decided to break in the process to her utter chagrin. She pushed inside, placing the suitcase next to its window. She dialled the number, but it didn't pick up. She tried her agent's office but was met with a stupid voicemail. Sighing, she put the phone back onto the hook of the metal banged up box and wrapped her arms around herself. "Well, I guess I have no other choice, but to wait until the morning," she thought sadly as she kicked a chunk of dirt and a piece of thin glass out of the way and sat down. Closing her eyes, she did her best to imagine that she was in her nice, soft, fluffy double bed, in her beautifully spacious, sea-themed bedroom with candles and jasmine incense burning away into puffs of porcelain smoke. As her mind drifted further into her delicately sweet mirage, the sounds of a passing car, clacking heels and the occasional famished stray cat slipped away from her consciousness as exhaustion consumed her into its void.

Early the next morning during their dance practice Taeyang managed to slip away briefly from his manager whilst he went on a cigarette break. He went to the library using a shortcut to avoid being spotted by fans or the press. If his manager found him, then he, along with the other members of Dark Star Seven would be locked in their dorm for a few days with nothing to do and not much to eat, which was always demeaning. He booted up the dated computer, he typed in the email, and did his best to explain the situation to this author. His spoken English was perfect, but his written English required improvement. Rubbing the back of his neck he admired his handiwork for a minute. With that done, he hit 'send', and leaned against the swivel chair he was sitting on before letting out a sigh.

Taeyang double-checked everything before logging out. There were no guarantees that an overly zealous fan wasn't hanging around, so he always made sure that he wiped his information before leaving the library. A couple of young students chatting away passed by causing him to pull his hood up further covering his face. He looked at the manuscript sitting comfortably inside of his green canvas backpack. He managed to sneak a few pages this morning when he woke up, more pages than he thought he would, but Taeyang had to admit that the story was not only addictive. He wasn't a fiction person but the protagonist in it really resonated with him plus it was a nice distraction from the usual. He zipped up his bag, and practically sprinted out of the building after looking at the worn clock. His bathroom break was most definitely over now. He pulled out his phone texting the group chat hoping that one of them could buy him enough time before their manager returned.

Taeyang arrived at the massive studio, his light silver hoodie clinging to his chest, he smiled smugly when he saw that the back window was wide open for him. He jumped through the open window landing on Soon Woo, who quickly pushed him off, groaning unhappily at being used as a human cushion. Taeyang got up before removing his backpack from his shoulders, placing it gently onto the floor before peeling off his stinky hoodie which he casually dropped onto Soon Woo who tossed it over his head before kicking at his friend's good ankle. He easily missed, which caused them both to chuckle. Their antics were interrupted when Hyeon handed Taeyang an open bottle of still water which he gratefully accepted. As he took a swig the metallic door rattled causing him to choke and drop the plastic bottle.

This caused Soon Woo to move so that water wouldn't splash onto him.

They all stiffened up as their manager eyed each one of them with distrust before turning his attention to the floor where the water had spilled and where the bottle was now lying. Taeyang bowed before fixing his shirt, the rest of the boys copying his actions except for Taemin who picked up the plastic bottle placing it into the bin before cleaning up the spilled liquid. Their manager glared at them before putting the music back on, and ordering the instructor to come back in. Taeyang kicked his backpack under the yellow wooden bleachers to ensure its safety before going back to their rigorous dance practice.

Autumn's face pressed against a hard, and weirdly wet surface. Her eyes fluttered open, the sudden light making them flinch. A headache sprouted across her brain as she pressed a tired hand against the glass in order to push herself onto her burning feet. She reached her shaky hand out struggling to move since her body was still heavy, and disjointed, partly from being in the recesses of sleep. Noises became clearer as vehicles screeched, along with the sounds of her own haggard breathing. The smell of roasting coffee from the nearby cafes shaking her senses back into life as the world resumed its ever-quickening pace. She gathered the first bit of energy she could grab before unhooking the phone and dialling a number. Hearing it ring she waited as she leaned against the green phone box trying to stay awake. Her muscles cramped, a burning sensation cutting at the fabric of her tendons as her balance tipped forward causing her to lean harder against the box. Just as the robotic voice of the machine answered her, she felt the presence of another. From the corner of her tired eye, she noticed a man approaching her; the sandalwood from his cologne wrapped around her throat like a cashmere scarf, bringing her numb body back to life.

Autumn smiled, her legs giving way with the turning up of her pale lips, her cheeks burned brightly at the man's subtle touch, her mind drawing a blank. Her thoughts became muddled as she tried to focus on him. The man had a dastardly handsome face with perfectly chiselled jaw and cheekbones, a craftmanship that only the gods themselves could have had. She then noticed his eyes. The darkened dying leaves of a million autumns, a thousand cups of roasted coffee and a hundred mysteries spiralling down a lonely bronze stairwell, that's what she could see inside of his large brown eyes as they pierced into her soul. In spite of her growing curiosity to discover more, she couldn't maintain her strength any longer as her ocean eyes rolled up into the back of her sockets; everything left her senses just as quickly as their brief interaction had been and she had no way of warning him as she fell from grace into the depths of sickly slumber.

Taeyang strolled back from the convenience store dusting off pieces of white rice from his long-sleeved navy-blue silk shirt. Following vocal practice, and a rather invasive interview about the group's upcoming plans for their tour this morning, he felt famished. Their schedule was lighter today, with only another dance practice later in the afternoon, a rare occurrence that he looked forward to whenever the opportunity came around. The clouds grumbled above him bringing his attention to the sky, as darkness overcame the city; the weather had been dismal all morning. He missed the vibrant sunshine, endless rain and wind weren't his thing.

Looking back to his surroundings there weren't a lot of people around, aside from two older school children passing him by in dark blue blazers carrying one instrument each. Taeyang continued walking when he spotted a woman inside of a green telephone box, she seemed oddly familiar to him. He deliberated for a moment; his bandmates were off doing their own thing for now, so he had time to kill for a change. Albeit that wasn't the only reason he was interested in her. The woman's unusual face caught his attention, it was a bit asymmetrical from the side yet fitted her chestnut hair and dainty shoulders perfectly, he paused in his steps to observe her further. The woman in question was lightly tanned, seemed to be a foreigner from what he could tell, looked dishevelled, of average height but still shorter than himself. She seemed to be distressed. Taeyang started walking towards her, "Why is she alone?" he asked in his head. South Korea is a safe place for the most part but he has heard stories about foreigners being assaulted especially women in the past.

Taeyang's eyes widened as he saw her visage up-close, her body appeared to be frail yet muscular and well-defined, it was apparent that this woman had slept rough – that is if she had slept at all, which he was starting to think that she hadn't. Her perfume invaded his senses causing his nose to twitch. A weird mixture of lavender and pine permeated his system. It reminded him of his halmeoni, she always wore obnoxious and ridiculous perfumes that made him want to gag. Taeyang also noticed that a suitcase like the one he had lost resided beside her feet that were being partly propped up by dirty and broken black stilettos. They looked to have seen better days. Autumn turned to look at him after she put the phone back on the hook, her expression was dazed initially. Her smile gleamed, their eyes locked in an instant. Taeyang gulped hard trying not to swallow his Adam's apple; her powder blue eyes held his attention as he noticed tinges of jade entwined around them. It was as if the whole universe existed within each layer of blue. He wasn't aware of how many seconds had passed between them during this exchange. But it didn't really matter to him as he noticed her eyes rolling back into her head as her body began wobbling.

The woman fell forward like a disgraced angel falling from heaven. In a flash, Taeyang had his arms wrapped protectively around her preventing her from face planting onto the gritty and unclean concrete. Her body's softness contradicted the taut muscles he could see in her arms and legs. He repositioned her in his arms to free his right hand, he held her limp wrist checking her pulse, her head lolled to the side. Autumn's heartbeat was slow but consistent. He sighed; her body felt cold to the touch but given what she was wearing that came as no surprise. He checked her forehead which was flaming hot with a raging fever as sweat started forming across her skin in beads. It didn't take a genius to figure out that she must have spent the night here. Taeyang placed her body in an upright position and sat her gently against the phone box. He licked his dry lips trying to think of something. For once, he was a bit lost for words. Here he was just out to enjoy the day.

Now, he has to deal with an unconscious woman he just met who has his suitcase. Taeyang went from licking his lips to biting them as he noticed more people starting to walk around. He had to get her out of here before a fan or a member of the press spotted him. He yanked out his phone from his pocket, he opened his most recent group chat, and texted the group the code "PURPLE." They had an agreement that if any of them ever got into a really bad situation then they would text this code, and whenever it was used, they all had to come running without question. Until they arrived, he stood vigil next to her sleeping form hoping that no one would recognise him.

Hyeon, and Soon Woo arrived briskly with no sign of the others.

"Where are they?" he barked.

The two of them shrugged.

Taeyang rolled his eyes mentally vowing to give the other members hell later on.

Hyeon noticed the luggage and looked between the unconscious woman and his leader.

"Isn't that your suitcase?" he asked, to which Taeyang nodded.

He was about to ask another question when he was cut off.

"So, why is she passed out?" Soon Woo interjected, receiving a shrug in exchange.

"I just approached her and then she fainted." Taeyang explained to them as he tried to figure out where to take her.

Hyeon spoke once again breaking up his thought process. "What do we do now Tae? Do we go or what?"

Taeyang just scratched his head looking at Autumn's prone form.

"We can't simply leave her here. Someone might see and I don't need a dead girl ruining my reputation, so let's just get her out of here," he stated, before scooping up her limp body into his arms.

Hyeon looked around briefly before giving him a quick thumbs up. He held her face against his chest then pointed to his suitcase. Hyeon sighed before retrieving the suitcase whilst Soon Woo kept looking around in a jittery manner trying to not draw any unwanted attention.

Once, they were out of view and away from anyone that could overhear them they paused. Taeyang rearranged Autumn onto his back. His hand brushed against her cheek; his eyebrows creased together feeling her face again before quickly pulling his free hand away. The fever burning her skin kept rising and if this continued then she could die. His chest tightened at that since he really didn't need a dead girl on his conscience; he secured her body before going over to Hyeon who was watching them with tense jade eyes. If she became any hotter, she was at risk of a febrile seizure or worse and there wasn't a hospital nearby to treat her. He thought it over for a minute before giving Soon Woo an order.

A few silent minutes passed before Soon Woo returned with a large sized iced water giving his friend a skeptical look. He removed her from his back pulling her body to his front. He took the drink from his friend's hand and put it onto the ground. He pulled off a piece of his shirt, digging out a few ice cubes from the drink causing it to drip over the plastic cup before wrapping the ice cubes into the torn material to create an ice pack of sorts. He tied it into a knot before he pushed it against her forehead, gesturing with his eyes towards the nearby alleyway. They awkwardly manoeuvered into the alleyway with Hyeon stuck carrying the suitcase.

Soon Woo glared at Taeyang as his back clipped against a very grimy dumpster. Taeyang mouthed something in Korean along the lines of "Grow up," before leading them farther away. He informed them that he'd go back to the dorm using a couple of shortcuts he knew about. Taking her body within his arms once more he cradled her close, her face looked peaky, and her hair was sticking to her skin as he continued pressing the icepack against her forehead. She was completely out of it, not even letting out a moan. Her breathing was laboured which made him nervous, but he needed to get her onto a bed, under proper lighting before he could fully assess the situation. He instructed Hyeon and Soon Woo to go get the others and meet him back at the dorm. They nodded, giving each other a concerned look before their eyes fell to Autumn. "She'll be fine just get going," he reassured them.

The two departed, leaving him with Autumn and the suitcase. Taeyang sighed, this would make carrying her tricky so as delicately as he could he placed her onto a clear patch on the ground before facing away from her. Stepping back, he crouched down, skilfully he used his hands to hoist her body up against his back flinching a little as his wrist twinged.

Taeyang carried Autumn on his back walking as briskly as he could as he juggled her and his suitcase. They couldn't stay gathered in public for too long or they'd risk being spotted, then chased by fans, and subsequently punished by their manager. He shivered at the image of his manager taking their real phones as well as cancelling their next album before indebting them financially all over again. After all, it took them three years to pay off the last one. They made it to the car park of their dorm. Both Hyeon, and Soon Woo had agreed to retrieve the others and meet him back here but what they didn't know was that they were all in for a telling off of an absolute lifetime once they were all gathered. Autumn's slipping body brought him back to the present. He halted his movements, letting go of the suitcase, he rearranged her body so that she was attached to his front. Clenching his teeth slightly, the pain in his wrist rearing its ugly head again. Using his arm, he held her to his muscular chest, whilst using the other hand to carry the suitcase. They entered the old building without hassle or being spotted; the backway stairs were a bit rickety, but he had conquered them without injury to Autumn, the suitcase, or himself.

In the dorm, Autumn resembled a masterful piece of hand sculpted clay as she lay on the bottom of a narrow bunk bed. A drenched blue cloth splayed across her forehead as she twitched and softly moaned in her sleep. Taeyang had checked her wallet to find out more details about her. It must be the woman who wrote the manuscript since the name was the same. He looked over the details scribbled in English before placing it back into her thin dress pocket. "So, you're the author," he thought to himself. Once the others arrived, Taeyang took great pleasure in yelling, and demeaning them for not responding to his emergency text and after a few lame excuses like 'my phone wasn't charged', 'I was busy', he dismissed his bandmates.

Then shifted back his attention on this woman before him. He took the liberty of discarding her very dirty and torn coat and busted shoes before checking over his own suitcase, nothing was taken or tampered with to his surprise and relief. Once he was done with that, he retrieved an icepack from the fridge before nursing his sore wrist and ankle intermittently. Tiredness hit his body like a freight train as he pressed the pack harder against his skin. A sharp knocking at the door alerted him as Hyeon entered, a merry smile splayed across his features.

"Hey Taeyang, how's our patient doing?" he asked, optimism shining through his voice.

Taeyang shrugged as he removed the icepack from his ankle placing it onto the windowsill before standing up. They stood in silence for a while. Hyeon checked her temperature again and suggested that they go to a hospital if it doesn't get any lower soon, but Taeyang was against it. It would create needless chaos. She had a moderate fever caused by staying out all night with insufficient outerwear. He shook his head looking at her. "Idiot, you've caused so much trouble," he remarked in his thoughts, watching the methodical rise and fall of her chest.

"What's her name anyway?" Hyeon asked Taeyang.

"Autumn - she is the owner of the bra you were dangling yesterday," he responded.

At this Hyeon blushed and turned his attention back to Autumn.

Her tanned hue flooded back into her cheeks as she remained still. A blanket had been haphazardly draped over her body. Hyeon sat at the end of the bed looking between Taeyang and the girl. Taeyang got up from his spot before pacing the room. He had expected her to be awake by now, but two hours had passed with no sign of her rousing. On top of that, the boys' dancing session was set for twenty minutes from now. One of them would have to fake being sick, they couldn't risk their manager finding an unconscious girl in their room. It would raise rather distasteful questions that none of them had answers for so with a nod to himself, he retrieved his phone from his pocket to text

Soon Woo instructing him to pull a sicky just for today. He shifted his focus back to the girl before vocalizing his decision.

"We'll keep her here until she wakes up, just throw the cover over her for now and make sure her head is covered just in case anyone comes in,"

Hesitantly, Hyeon leaned slowly over to her side pulling the soft blanket over her body until her face had been covered.

He whispered softly to her, "Sweet dreams, sweet Autumn," before getting up and carefully closing over the door as he left.

Chapter Two

The Idol Treatment

Autumn jumped upright on the bed, her head brushed against the underside of the top bunk. She felt a cotton blanket slip from her chest onto her lap; her ears were buzzing and ringing as the heavy shackles on her mind were melting into oblivion. Her memories flashed before her in pieces resembling fragments of a broken mirror.

"Those brown eyes..." she gasped to the empty room.

She rubbed her stiff eyes with her free hand before panic sunk in, she had no idea where she was, in a foreign country, and she hadn't been able to get through to her agent to explain what was holding her up. Her alarm grew massively when she heard high-pitched giggling coming from the ajar closet. Her throat constricted as panic began settling into her bones. She stood but was still a little wobbly on her feet and approached the closet slowly. She was a foot away when it happened. A rumble blared from behind the wooden doors before a short girl popped out flashing a camera. Autumn stumbled back blinking rapidly as shock and surprise filled her body. She couldn't scream, she could only dumbly blink as this strange girl slinked out of the room with a finger pressed against her cracked pink lips. "What the hell was that?" Autumn thought as she stared at the door the girl had exited through.

After a few minutes, though, she felt calm enough to analyse her surroundings.

"Is this a dorm?" Autumn asked aloud as she looked around the room.

The wooden bunk beds sat opposite each other with a small cedar desk at the bottom on the left-hand side of the room next to what appeared to be an old and overused closet. The bedroom appeared childlike in its size with painted walls and a set of open and worn emerald curtains barely touching the floor. As she felt the hazel coloured wood against her feet, she noticed that her shoes had been taken off, but she couldn't spot them anywhere and that her coat was nowhere to be seen either. "How strange!" she thought.

As she got a better look around, she noticed a cheap wooden picture frame on the small bedside table. She picked it up, before examining it. In the picture, stood a little boy smiling, holding a fish on a line. Engraved were the words 'Taeyang Chan'. Her mind pondered over his name. The door opened abruptly startling Autumn who dropped the picture frame. The man from before had entered the room. "This must be Taeyang," she deduced looking him over as he gave her an unamused glance in return. She broke out of her stupor when she noticed his stare shifting to her uncovered feet. She gasped, remembering the frame. Looking down she was relieved to discover that there were no marks or a crack on the glass. Picking it up she placed it back onto its original position on the nightstand before taking another look at Taeyang.

Upon getting a better look at the man this time, she had to admit she was impressed. Taeyang appeared to be about six feet tall, a faded scar marked his right hand, his hair was dyed royal blue with a silver streak running through it. His lips were slightly cracked but a pleasant shade of peachy pink and quite plump, he had a habit of licking them ever so often. She found this endearing until he opened his mouth to speak.

"Where is Soon Woo? I instructed him to babysit you until we came back!" he snapped in English.

Before Autumn had a chance to answer he continued...

"Well, sleeping beauty, did you enjoy hogging my bed and almost getting me fired?"

The anger in voice increasing with every syllable.

"Or was stealing my luggage just an excuse to meet me? International stalker fan? Or are you really an author or just some airhead who gets off stealing?" he bombarded her.

Taeyang found her lack of response annoying. Was she dumb or something?

She stood there with her mouth resembling that of a freshly caught trout before her mind caught up.

"You speak English?" she questioned which caused him to roll his eyes indignantly.

"Out of everything that I just said, that's the part you're picking up on?! Maybe the exposure did damage your brain after all. You, stupid foreigner," he snapped the last part in Korean feeling thoroughly insulted by her shock at his ability to speak another language.

Autumn opened her mouth to say something quippy, insulting, anything that would knock off the smirk that was forming across his face at her dumbfoundedness, yet the words were hindered inside of her tired throat. He laughed coldly at this, folding his arms as he did so. Maybe the cold had screwed up her mind just a little bit.

"For an author, you aren't very good with words," he said delivering another blow to her crumbling self-esteem.

In that moment she didn't know what to do. Everything hit her. Everything felt overwhelming. She couldn't even verbalise anything. Her chest tightened. She was far from home in a place where nothing made sense to her. Being dealt insults by a strange man who seemed like an absolute dick. It was intense. She didn't know what to do. She just couldn't handle anymore.

Autumn did something that caught him unawares, she started to cry. His smirk faltered upon seeing tears fall down her reddening face and hearing the exhausted cries that started to emerge from her mouth. He panicked, he wanted to get her angry not reduce her into a crying mess.

"L-look um, I was just kidding, I've read your manuscript it wasn't that bad. Stop crying," he clumsily spluttered out.

Sadly, this provoked her further as her crying became loud sobs, she kept her head down. Taeyang looked around the room for something to help him, aside, from the colourful plushies on the other beds there wasn't anything he could give her to calm her down, so he did the next best thing. He walked up to her and poked her shoulder. This caused her to freeze before looking up. Her face resembled a cherry tomato, clear snot trickled from her nose a little bit as her eyes were glassy with water. He sighed, before leaning over to the nightstand. He opened the drawer and retrieved a clean white hanky. He reluctantly wiped her face with it before gently stuffing it into her hand and closing it over.

"Look, we can't risk you being seen here because our managers will go crazy if they see you. I'll explain things later. For now, calm down and go freshen up." he said.

Autumn nodded, trying to calm herself down before asking,

"W-where's the bathroom?"

He sighed, and pointed towards the door at the bottom of the room near the bunkbeds.

"Thanks," she whimpered before trudging towards it.

Autumn's mind still felt confused and overwhelmed. It was at least comforting to know that there was someone here who could speak her language. Once she was inside, she examined the bathroom; it was spotless which was surprising since so many people used it on a frequent basis. There was a lack of space, with the shower and the toilet being just a foot from each other. All white porcelain, with a clear shelf above the toilet. The drain for the shower was also bigger than she had expected but unfortunately had black hair in it which made her gag slightly. The room was a complete contrast from her bathroom in her home back in Canada that had two sinks and enough space for four to use comfortably in one sitting. She checked the beige plastic cabinets that had golden stubs for handles; the shelves were covered with used skincare products, and body colognes which were sitting in various positions. She took a sniff at the amber bottle and grimaced before she closed over the doors. The scent made nausea bubble in her gut; the muskiness of the scent was disgustingly potent and cruelly invasive. "That must be Taeyang's," she thought to herself.

From numerous videos she had seen online in the past she knew that there were certain things foreigners had to lookout for here. One

24

of them being hidden cameras. She checked the silver screws of the door handle before checking the toilet seat. Hidden cameras were even found in some public toilets here, so Autumn checked thoroughly to ensure that she had not missed anything.

"Looking for something?" an irritated voice suddenly spoke causing her to jump up.

"I-I," she stammered, fumbling with her hands.

Taeyang stared her down for a moment, gaining some satisfaction that he could make her squirm easily with his mere presence.

"Our toilets are a little different. That nozzle is to clean your butt," Taeyang said pointing to the metallic nozzle that sat erect in the toilet.

She looked at him astonished by his crudeness.

He laughed.

"What's wrong? Does the idea of cleaning your butt scare you that much?" he taunted.

"N-no! It's just a more unusual thing in the west...t-the butt-keister-washer thing, not cleaning your behind," she told him as her cheeks burned with a mixture of embarrassment and anger.

"Tch. Foreigners." he muttered in Korean before laughing, she truly was something else.

After nothing but silence lingered between the two, he decided to provoke her more, so he poked her face snapping her out of the daze that she was in; her eyes were doe like under the yellowish strip bathroom lights.

"Do you have a brain problem? You keep staring and saying nothing. It's weird," he stated.

At this Autumn glared wanting to smack him but she was shattered.

"You're saying that as if you are the height of human intellect," she countered.

"Well, my height is still above yours, so," he jabbed.

She rolled her eyes at that. He was being annoying and it wasn't cute. Taeyang noticed how tired and fed up she looked. He decided to switch the subject.

"Look, Soon Woo was meant to fake being sick to look after you. I don't know where he is, but I've got to go back to practice. Once, we are finished, me, and a couple of others from our group will be returning. Until we get this mess straightened out, I insist that you stay in our room,"

This caused her to liven up as she looked into his eyes. Her fear and nervousness were off the charts.

"But I need to contact my agent. I have a deadline-" Autumn tried to explain.

Imploring him to reconsider with her slightly bloodshot eyes.

"It can wait. Just stay here and don't make tons of noise because if you do, we are all toast. So, don't do anything stupid!" he warned her emphasizing his point with his finger before he walked away.

Her fear quickly turned into anger. The nerve of him wanting to keep her here. It's not her fault that he decided to basically kidnap her. But saying that, he had helped her shake her fever, and he didn't try to harm her. Plus, he is the only one here that she can talk to. Literally.

After deliberating, she decided to play along for now until she could get out of this jam with her manuscript and things intact. Until then she decided to investigate the room to see if he had planked her manuscript somewhere. She searched her suitcase first; her clothes and essentials were inside (granted they had been tampered with by the looks of it – to her annoyance), but her beloved manuscript was gone. Autumn bit her lip holding back a frustrated scream. Her deadline loomed above her head, in the same way that the darkening clouds casted ugly shadows across Seoul's streets, and glittering skyscrapers today. She sighed at the open yet lifeless suitcase mocking her as she sat there looking at its barren folds. After berating herself mentally for a little while she went for the door, but it was locked. She huffed in indignation.

"What am I supposed to do? And how am I supposed to call my agent?" she spoke, wringing her hands until they were pink. Her anxiety flaring up.

She knew that people, mainly her agent and publisher, would start worrying about her absence which made her feel upset since she didn't like to rock the boat or cause problems. Especially with her bosses.

Autumn couldn't see her manuscript anywhere, so she gave up and decided to climb onto the top bunk of one of the beds before jumping onto it, the mattress bounced slightly sending the purple comforter to the ground. She lay down staring at the ceiling. Each swirl of plaster resembled vast unruly waves of an angered sea. She covered her eyes as she exhaled deeply. Being confined to this room brought back memories of her own childhood. The world seemed to blur out as she remembered those darker times. Autumn had been just five years old when her father had died. He was a sweet man who struggled, battled, went from rehab clinic to five step programmes in his fight to overcome his alcohol addiction but in the end, his demons had consumed him. After his passing, she was put into the care of her cruel cousin who made her run the house whilst he went off and did, God only knows what. Autumn used writing to cope with her circumstances and before she knew it, she had fallen in love with the craft. She daydreamed about writing some more before she fell asleep.

Several hours had passed with no sign of anyone's return. She woke up feeling better than she had earlier. Stretching her body, her bones cracked slightly. Her stomach erupted with a growl. Autumn felt famished since she hadn't eaten in over twenty-four hours. She prayed that the boys would return before she starved to death. She climbed down from the bed and decided to search the drawers hoping for a piece of chocolate or a snack bar hidden somewhere. Aside from clothes and notebooks, there wasn't anything edible just a Choco pie wrapper. This burned her up since she absolutely loved anything chocolate related. Shoving the drawer shut she huffed as her stomach growled unhappily once more.

Taeyang, Hyeon, and Soon Woo entered the room. Autumn sat on the floor stewing in her emotions whilst holding her very hungry and sore stomach.

Taeyang raised an eyebrow at that, "Autumn, get up and stop cluttering the floor," he said shaking his head

She narrowed her eyes at him before practically jumping up to meet his gaze.

"Look, Taeyang, I've been stuck inside of this room for hours. There's no food, or anything to do. PLUS, you're one to talk about clutter when you have a bunch of fan girls living in your closet!" she snapped before poking his chest.

He rolled his eyes until the last part registered with him.

"What girls?" he asked, his lips were tight, but the glint of fear in his eyes told her that he was genuinely confused and concerned.

"When I woke up earlier, I heard giggling coming from your closet. When I opened it, two girls came out. One had a camera and had the audacity to flash it in my face!" she relayed to him removing her finger from his chest.

He cursed under his breath and muttered something in Korean to Hyeon and Soon Woo causing them to bow to her before leaving.

She looked at him as concern began clouding her own features, her hunger was forgotten for now.

"So, what was that about? Why did they have to leave? What did you say?" she asked him.

He gestured to the bed not looking at her directly in the eyes.

"How did they get in? When did they get in?" These questions echoed in his mind. It was always the same.

She sat down twiddling her fingers as she observed Taeyang who seemed somewhat lost in his own head as he sat beside her.

"If what you're saying is true-" Taeyang started but Autumn interjected

"It is!" she crossed her arms.

"Rude much? What I am SAYING is that if there were girls in the closet you should forget about them, they aren't worth the headspace," he finished mulling over the situation.

"What do you mean?" Autumn enquired but he looked very uncomfortable at this point.

Taeyang was fidgeting with a silver ringer that was on his finger and his body was pointing slightly away from her.

"How are you feeling?" he asked changing the subject before she could ask anything else.

Although the change in topic was annoying, although he was annoying, if it made him this uncomfortable to go further into it then maybe it was best for her to leave it alone.

Taeyang watched her, waiting for answer.

Looking at him, she thought about how she felt. Her body felt sore and she was starving. But she didn't feel ill like before. But burning out came as no surprise to her when she thought about her life. Managing on five hours of sleep most days whilst she tried to finish her latest novel. She just adored her job, it was her life, her reason for being and her fans were like her children, but she struggled to balance her career and personal life. Most of the time, they merged into each other or collided. Her expression became crestfallen as she thought about her personal life more specifically. Autumn didn't want to go further into this subject.

"I'm fine. Thanks," she responded before getting up to use the restroom.

"Liar," he mumbled as he watched her leave.

She caught a glimpse of herself in the mirror and turned up her nose at her appearance. Traces of charcoal eyeliner coated the corners of her eyes. Her eyebrows looked a tad untamed and downtrodden, and her skin had traces of powdery foundation on it. Her hair resembled an oily film sitting on top of manure.

"Where's dry shampoo when you need it?" she thought miserably.

With everything that had happened, she wanted to at least do something relaxing. Turning on the tap she gathered water within the palms and splashed it against her face. The coolness of the liquid felt pleasurable against her stuffy skin. The remnants of her make-up poured into the drain. Sweet relief filled her as she became free from that disgustingly caked foundation and her skin was finally able to breathe. Taking another look, she smiled, her face looked glassy apart from a few white heads on her forehead. That's the upside of being in this strange country; every product known to man that could fix a person's skin existed here. It was amazing. Then just as luck would have it, she came across a few protein bars as she looked for a sponge to clean up the sink.

Once Autumn refreshed herself, she re-entered the room to find Taeyang chilling on his bed. She went with the direct approach about something that had been bugging her.

"Taeyang, where is my manuscript? And by the way I ate some of the protein bars in the bathroom."

He responded with a shake of his head

"And I don't care about the protein bars. You were hungry. It's fine,"

"Thanks. Now can I have my manuscript please?" she tried again.

"No," he replied not wanting to move

"Come on, Taeyang. Where is it?" she asked folding her arms

"Somewhere," he retorted nonchalantly as he played with his hands.

"Taeyang..." she said, anger rising in her voice

"Autumn..." he mocked, putting his hands down.

"Give me my manuscript. Or I will cut your testicles off," she warned him narrowing her cobalt eyes.

He rolled his eyes at that. If she wasn't being so ridiculous he would find it cute. Standing there with her arms crossed and her lip pouted like an indignant trout.

"You want to cut my manhood over a manuscript? The fact that you think that you could is cute but watch it. I give as good as I get, foreigner," he responded narrowing his eyes at her.

Autumn's eyes widened at that as she covered her chest with her arms.

As fun as torturing Autumn was, the manuscript was her property and he needed to give it back.

He laughed before dragging himself off of the bed.

"I will not give you your manuscript until you prove something to me," he told her matter-of-factly.

She rolled her eyes at him but decided to go along with this for the sake of her book.

"Fine. Go on," she told him gesturing with her hand

"In the first line of the third paragraph, what does the character grapple with?" he quizzed her.

She tapped her cheek before her eyes lit up. "She's grappling with the death of her ex-boyfriend whilst dealing with the conflicting feelings of guilt and love she feels for the man she met in the evergreen woods," she answered giving him a smirk.

He clapped slowly.

"You passed, congrats, idiot," he remarked going before her to flick her nose.

She held her nose, glaring at him as her smirk vanished. "What did you do that for eh?" she asked, her voice muffled by her hand.

"There's only room for one ego. Remember that, Autumn," he stated, smirking as she rubbed her nose.

She didn't give him the satisfaction of reacting any further, so she buried her rising temper and the compulsion to break his smug little neck down into her core.

"Can we please go get my manuscript now? Or do I have to carry out my threat?" she asked making scissor gestures with her hand.

He scoffed at her feeble attempt to be intimidating but relented since he didn't want to push his luck.

"It's at the dance studio, so let's go get your silly manuscript, before I change my mind," he said.

She nodded eagerly before dashing out of the room until she realised something....

"Where is the dance studio and can I have some shoes?" she asked as she took a few steps back causing him to tut before he pointed left and pulled out a pair of white sneakers from the closet.

Sometimes Taemin's younger sister would come over and she had the same size feet as Autumn. They seemed to fit well as she put them on.

"Thanks, Taeyang," she said merrily as she slipped the shoes on.

She was all smiles as she skipped off. He rolled his eyes slightly smiling as he watched her rush off ahead of him.

Chapter Three

Falling Flowers, And Stalker Fans

Under the cover of darkness, Taeyang closely followed by Autumn, travelled to the studio where he had forgotten his bag. She took a peep into the pristine window; the lights were off, and the room was vacant. He pushed up the window, it creaked a little before opening. She had to wait outside just to make sure that no one would catch them and make the wrong assumption. He made his way inside; the place was empty, sure enough. He lurked about using his flashlight to get a better look. He stubbed his right foot on a chair that had been left out, and groaned with water brimming in his chocolate eyes. Autumn remained still as she kept an eye out hoping that they could get this whole thing done and over with so that she could go home and pretend that none of it ever happened.

Taeyang searched his bag for the manuscript.

He tossed the bag cursing, "Damn these fucking Sasaengs!"

This alarmed Autumn outside as she whispered, "Taeyang? Are you okay?"

He didn't respond but appeared a few seconds later. He rushed out of the window, fire bristling brightly in his chestnut eyes. He grasped Autumn's hand pulling her along without saying a word. She shivered; chills waltzed across her spine as her feet dragged against the hard concrete. Heat cascaded over her cheeks, his hand moving roughly against her own. Moonlight reflecting off his porcelain cheeks, it gave him an ethereal aura that had her transfixed and practically drooling.

"No. He's a douche, Autumn. But I must admit that he is kind of cute," she thought to herself.

Taeyang, on the other hand, was flustered and somewhat ticked off, he had lost Autumn's manuscript, and there was no doubt in his mind that the girls who had been following them were behind it. On top of that, if the media got wind of this then it could start an unnecessary yet large scandal which would ruin all of their careers. He had enough rumours flying around about him like that one about him hooking up with a trainee from a completely different company.

Autumn was brought back to reality and anger by a mosquito flying into her face. She used her free hand to rub the spot that the putrid little creature had touched, in disgust, before she redirected her attention to Taeyang. Yanking her hand away she refused to budge any further.

"I want an explanation. Where is my manuscript? And you still haven't explained those girls from before. Who are they? And give me an actual answer this time, Taeyang," she demanded, folding her arms.

Taeyang turned to look at her, noting how royally ticked off she looked even in the dark, her anger was palpable.

He sighed. "Look, I'm sorry but those girls have stolen your manuscript. Which I may add, that you lost in the first place because you chose to put in it your luggage. That aside, I've been the one wasting my precious time looking after it as well as looking for it. You should be grateful that an idol like me would help you at all," he said before looking arrogantly at her.

Her fists were clenched, her blue eyes grew stormy with a darker navy hue swishing around them.

"Help me? By kidnapping me? Taeyang, I don't want your apology... but I want my manuscript back, and I want to know just why those two girls have it!" she seethed as her anger began to spill over.

He rolled his eyes at the kidnapping remark but laughed at the display of anger.

"Those girls are called Sasaengs, they stalk idols, and do basically anything to gain their attention. Some even resort to hiding in dorms, like you saw today." he explained as his eyes darkened at that.

She gasped in disbelief, he tried to push it down, but pain and a hint of embarrassment laced his words.

"Sae-what?" she asked but he held up his hand.

"Just stalker fans. But the point is that I don't have your manuscript," he replied.

"I'm sorry that you have to deal with that," Autumn said as her anger began fizzling out.

The weight of this information sat on her shoulders. Guilt started to replace anger. She was so busy worrying about her book that she didn't think about how this would affect Taeyang.

"I chose this life, and the baggage that comes with it so don't waste your apology on me," Taeyang snapped, feeling unsettled by the look of guilt in her eyes.

"Regardless, we need to get it back. My deadline is in two days, and if I'm not in Canada, I might as well as be floating in the Han River." she deadpanned when the silence started to become uncomfortable between them.

Autumn was afraid. If she didn't obtain her book in time then her publisher may drop her altogether. Since she has witnessed this happen to other successful authors in the past.

Taeyang gave her a once-over. She really needed to get changed out of those ugly clothes and she seemed so worried. It angered him how worked up she made herself but he didn't understand why. "It's not like it will appear if she stresses out like this, it's like she wants to make herself sick," he thought to himself. He watched her for a couple of more minutes before an idea entered his head and he stole her hand, dragging her close behind him. They passed through each dirty, cramped and downright sleazy alleyway until he pulled Autumn behind a large, overflowing dumpster. The smell coming from it was absolutely putrid.

"What are you doing?" she whispered frantically trying not to throw up.

Taeyang shushed her, two girls came into view. Both were dressed in black overcoats, one of them was holding a tape recorder. After his many dealings with them, he knew where these kinds of people tended to frequent. He figured that if he was right, then there would be a chance that he could retrieve Autumn's manuscript. Taeyang crouched, pushing her closer to the wall behind the dumpster. She cringed; the alleyway had discarded tissues along with a clear mysterious liquid substance littering the ground.

"Talk about disgusting." she sneered in her thoughts at the ugly sight.

Taeyang took baby steps in approaching the two women, Autumn stayed back somewhat confused by his actions. She also bit her tongue trying not to yell at him to hurry up before the smell of the fermenting dumpster suffocated her. She did her best to keep her balance as she watched him greet the mysterious women.

The distance between her spot and where Taeyang stood was too far away to hear the conversation, plus she didn't speak much Korean which didn't help but using her deduction skills she guessed that whatever did transpire would lead them closer to finding her manuscript.

He knew from the minute they had spotted him that something was off. Aside from the fact that were wearing overcoats in Korea which was only a thing in winter. They were conversing in hushed tones in an empty street, in the middle of the night. These two certainly weren't the brightest of the crazy bunch. He enacted his best smooth look for the ladies' face that he stole from Soon Woo. "This better work," he thought bitterly.

One of them gave him a sweet smile that made his lips turn up in disdain. The other one was twitchy and barely spoke as she avoided eye contact. He managed to figure out the situation in record time as he conversed with them, now it was time to take action before this crazed nonsense carried on any further.

Swiping the tape recorder from her hand he examined it. It had hours' worth of recordings. He slipped it into his pocket.

"You two should go. Now," he spat as he glared at the two.

The taller one was about to protest but the look in his eyes said it all. She receded into her jacket, her form quivering under his intense look of disgust.

Taeyang removed his phone from his pocket and started texting the rest of the group. It took a lot of restraint for him not to knock those sasaengs onto their behinds.

"You can come out now," he spoke to Autumn who was still standing in the alleyway.

She walked toward him, relieved to be a good distance from the stinky dumpster, and grubby alley.

"So, did you find out anything?" she questioned, standing a couple of inches from him.

His cologne invaded her senses, the top notes were sandalwood and Allspice, which made her stomach flutter. Something about those scents felt familiar.

"Nothing of interest, just a tape recorder but...I will deal with that later," he revealed, an ominous look on his face.

Autumn slowly nodded not quite believing him but decided to leave it for now. He tugged on her hand. "We shouldn't hang around here for too long. It's not the safest area." he spoke with urgency.

"Right," she said as she allowed herself to be pulled behind him as they headed off.

They sat on the roof watching the stars that twinkled over the valley. Taeyang had bought them some dinner. He knew that he should have been back at the dorm, but he wanted time to figure things out. Autumn had been silent since their trip to the convenience store. He chewed absentmindedly on his steak sandwich. She observed him whilst eating her rice ball. He was a strange individual, his personality was questionable yet there was a deeper layer, a glimmer of compassion mixed with empathy. Annoyingly, that part of him was overshadowed by his ego, a pendulum encased in stone walls as high as the Jeongbang Waterfall.

Autumn sat closer to him; she wasn't sure what to say. She wanted to know more about him, but she didn't want to pry into anything overly personal.

"What do you want to ask?" he directed at her.

She felt chills once again, as he locked eyes with her.

"How did he know?" she thought to herself giving him a slightly baffled look.

Taeyang shook his head laughing at her silly expression.

"Well, I was wondering, you seem to dislike being idol. So, why don't you just quit?" she asked playing with her hands.

"I trained for years before I debuted. To work hard like that and then quit would be an insult to everyone who has ever believed in me," he confessed, his eyes becoming an inferno as he recalled every sacrifice, every missed birthday, every spoiled friendship that had occurred because of his training and subsequently his idol status. She stared at him, he was a grossly cocky individual yet when he talked openly like this, it was clear that being an idol had taken its toll over the years.

"Since you don't know, your face bleeds your thoughts clearly," Taeyang stated smirking, as he responded to her unaired thought.

Autumn blushed. "Jerk," she mumbled trying to come up with a witty retort.

She placed her chin into her hands thinking about the last few hours.

"So, what's with the ring on your finger?" she asked pointing at his hand.

Taeyang scoffed. "It was my uncle's. It's a good luck charm, I've never performed without it," he informed her, ignoring her awestruck stare.

"Why did you put your zodiac sign on your suitcase?" Taeyang asked, adjusting the ringer on his forefinger.

Autumn yawned, turning her head away.

"Well, I am a Pisces, so it made sense to put something personal on my suitcase, so I'd never lose it," she responded.

Taeyang rolled his eyes tutting, "Yeah, because that worked out so well for you, didn't it, leafy?"

She stuck her tongue out at Taeyang and the nickname. He smirked, shrugging his shoulders. A peaceful silence followed as they basked in the beauty of the constellations merging above their heads.

By the time Taeyang and Autumn returned to the dorm the lights were off, and the beds were full with a couple of members with the rest fast asleep in separate sleeping bags on the hardwood floor. She was zapped with guilt seeing the lack of space the boys were forced to share day in and day out. He poked her in the shoulder causing her to snap back into reality.

"Are you going in or not? We don't have all night, leafy," he said wanting her to hurry up.

She rolled her eyes at him before placing her hands onto the ledge and with the skill and grace of a limber cat she climbed through the open window. She slipped into the room tripping forward when Taeyang grabbed her dress pulling her back before she fell on top of Kim who was sleeping inside a red sleeping bag on the floor. She repressed a tremble as Taeyang's smooth skin clipped the top of her bare back.

Taeyang sat the end of the second bunk bed trying not to wake Hyeon who was clutching onto a pink plushie for dear life. Autumn cracked her back feeling the tension dissipate, between sleeping inside of a phone box and being on her feet for most of the day her back wasn't having any of it as each lumber ached and was stiff. She looked over at Taeyang who hadn't said a word thus far. He looked to her for a second before staring into space.

An awkward silence brewed between the duo. Then Autumn remembered her question from a while ago.

"Why do you guys sleep in a dorm anyway?" she asked looking at the cramped room with distaste.

Taeyang who licked his lips turning away, explained, "When we train for debut, the company pays for everything. You don't get a say on what's being used or who's being hired. It includes living expenses too."

She sighed, "But you've been debuted for years, isn't the debt paid off?" she enquired further. He looked toward the ceiling.

"That's the thing, each time we do a comeback, we either become indebted again or it is paid off. I could afford to buy my own place but I've lived here for so long now, living somewhere else would feel weird," he stated, shifting awkwardly where he sat.

"Ah, maybe that's why you're such a grumpy guy. You don't have your own space," she whispered before poking him lightly.

He glared at her before rolling his eyes.

"I rarely get more than four hours sleep, and my manager is always on my case. That's just the tip of the iceberg in my life right now," Taeyang revealed solemnly.

The playfulness died at that.

She mulled over his words, a deep sadness forming within the chambers of her heart upon hearing this revelation.

Autumn drifted off to sleep after a while. Taeyang draped a white blanket over her. She looked pathetically small, yet quite precious in this state. Her happiness radiated from her body even as she twitched and moved in her unconscious stupor. He shook his head, any other person would have punched him and went to the police, yet she actually listened to him and was going along with this despite not really knowing him. Somehow, she had chosen to overlook his faults and contend with him enough to want to know more about him. That in itself kind of amazed him.

Suddenly, a rather ugly snore caught his attention, he looked over, and laughed to himself upon seeing Hyeon snuggling with that godawful pink travesty he called a plushie. Getting up, he searched the desk before yanking out what he was looking for. He angled the device to get the perfect shot of Hyeon lovingly cuddling the plushie before clicking it and tossing the phone back into the desk to use as blackmail later. Soon Woo mumbled in his sleep, a vibrant reddish hickey on his neck that shone under the moonlight piercing through the glass of the window like a pilot light on an oil rig.

The room was out cold, which gave him the opportunity to indulge in personal time for a change. Before leaving the room, he wanted to check everything was in order, he closed the windows making sure that they were locked, turned up the heating to a nice and even temperature before waltzing off to the bathroom to pamper himself.

Taeyang left the shower, His blue locks still dripping by the time he returned to the room. The only light in the room illuminated from his phone that was vibrating on the table. He stepped over Autumn's sleeping figure before answering his phone. He growled after hanging up, his manager Chen was always harassing him over something silly. He really wanted to punch him sometimes. If he wasn't overscheduling him then he was dictating him about how to live his personal life. Taeyang rubbed his temple furiously trying to combat the migraine that was sneaking its way across his brain.

Taeyang paused, looking at Autumn's dozing form. Her nose twitched, eliciting a small smile from the otherwise frustrated Taeyang. Her thick chestnut hair lay perfectly. Even the stale pong of her floral perfume didn't irritate his senses to the same degree that it had earlier. But he put that down to them being outside for so long that the smell of pollution dimmed its potency considerably. Taeyang went into their kitchen, he checked the fridge and found some leftovers. He sighed before removing them and dumping it into the trash. Taeyang liked to keep order, and the dorm somewhat hygienic. Two-day old leftovers would cause a stench he didn't feel like being yelled at by Chen over. Once he did that, he went over to their coffee machine. Taeyang popped in an espresso pod from the glass jar and set-up the machine. Taeyang then grabbed a fresh pink sponge from the soapy basin and wiped the countertops down.

His mind drifted back to Autumn, it was strange how she could go from a sleepy weakling to a nosey, but nervous person all in one day. However, the look of pain that came over her face when he told her about the manuscript nagged him. It was as if that manuscript had an intrinsic meaning to her that she wasn't even aware of from what he'd seen. Then again, if it were him in that situation, he'd probably feel the same. Over three hundred pages, that's a feat few accomplish, and some do with the knowledge that it may never see the light of day. A beeping brought him back to the present. The coffee was ready, so he finished up cleaning before grabbing his drink and leaving. Taeyang opted for the living room to chill since he had a better view of the starry sky shimmering through the half-covered windows. He sipped on his cup of coffee whilst his mind drifted deeper into his growing concerns; sleep would not come to him on this night.

Hyeon was the first to greet Taeyang as he entered the living room. Taeyang grunted, sinking further into the leather couch. His joints were giving him grief this morning. His ankle wasn't as bad today, ironically, but he still wasn't joyous about feeling like a door that needed a good oiling. Taeyang closed his eyes giving himself a minute before facing the world. A pillow hitting his face made him expel a muffled groan. He opened his eyes in to face his annoyance only to be met by his friend's mischievous grin.

Autumn followed shortly after; she seemed refreshed and had a better bounce to her vibe this morning. However, her clothes looked grubbier than the day before. He internally groaned looking to the side before dragging himself up. Autumn looked at him curiously.

"Have you been up all night, Tae?" she asked her voice, laced with concern.

Taeyang brushed past her without a word. He needed a shower and didn't feel like talking.

"Must not be a morning person," she thought to herself before going to the kitchen where a caffeinated pick me up was waiting for her.

A few hours later...

Taeyang tapped his chin thoughtfully, the sasaengs had access to their dorm, and other places so that meant that there must be one of them on the inside; a rat so to speak. He was so lost in his musings that he didn't even notice the look that he was on the receiving end of from Autumn. She found his pensiveness interesting. As if he was trying to crack some ridiculously complicated code. It entertained her as they both sat on the crimson leather couch.

Hyeon who was sipping from a petite carton of strawberry milk gave Taeyang and Autumn the side-eye from his spot on the floor. Autumn just smiled his way; her teeth sparkled with an ivory glow as the odour of mint laced her breath. He smiled back giving her a little wave.

Taeyang looked her way for a minute before reaching down the side of couch, and pulling out a plastic purple bag. Autumn watched him peering over at the mysterious bag. He tapped her nose using his finger before placing the bag into her lap. She blinked, rubbing her nose whilst giving him a surprised stare. Carefully she touched the bag, Autumn marvelled at it. It glistened under the light and made a crackling noise as she moved it.

"What did he do this for?" she thought examining the bag now nestled on her lap. He bumped her shoulder gently,

"Open it, it's not going to explode," he told her trying to ease her concern.

She separated the two sides of the bag that had been clinging together. Her heart skipped as excitement waterfalled down her spine. Inside the bag were stylish work like dresses, Autumn looked to Taeyang who cleared his throat looking away.

"Your clothes resemble old curtains, and I'm sick of looking at them. They hurt my eyes," he told her truthfully, making a disgusted face.

Autumn smacked his chest lightly, but her smile never left her sweet cherry lips. Taeyang started rubbing his neck feeling uncomfortable.

"Look further inside," he instructed her.

Autumn tilted her head before pushing her hand lower into the bag. She felt two lumps of rubber, and smooth leather against her fingertips. She pulled them out carefully. Taeyang smirked as he watched her feeling the dimensions of the shoes as if she had never seen anything like it before. Autumn's smile widened as tears started to shimmer across her cobalt eyes. Taeyang didn't think it was possible for anyone to look captivating when they cried but somehow Autumn managed it with her eyes becoming a Mediterranean Sea that drowned him with ease. He blushed, looking away as she wrapped her arms around him.

"Thank you so much Taeyang! These are so awesome!" she exclaimed with a giggle, holding him close.

Taeyang's eyes widened as he tapped her back cautiously. He wasn't expecting this kind of reaction – not one bit. Autumn's cheeks burned into an inferno as hormones gushed through her. She was so swept up within her joy that she hadn't noticed how flustered he was becoming from the intimate contact.

Taeyang pushed her away gently. Being so close made him feel uncomfortable. Her heat felt electrifying to his skin that excitedly rose at the close contact only adding to his growing discomfort. Autumn's body brought up sensations he spent years locking away, deeming them as impulses of the primitive mind that would hinder his ascension to fame. Unlike, certain members of his group, who had girls and sex on the brain whenever they weren't on idol duty. It wouldn't even bother him if he didn't have to share a room with them. And hear those weird noises at ridiculously late hours. He scowled at the memory of a black bra flying onto his face as he got up to go use the bathroom. The ugly high-pitched giggling of that silly girl to whom it belonged to still made him sneer with absolute red-hot loathing.

Autumn changed into one of her new dresses and a pair of shoes. The material of the dress was a sheer black cotton that hugged her form nicely especially her hips. Taeyang blushed, sharply turning his head away as he saw it along with her wedged brown shoes. She looked sophisticated. Alluring and somewhat dangerous. How a woman like herself should look. Hyeon put down his now virtually empty strawberry milk winking at Taeyang who gave him a suggestion with his middle finger. Hyeon smirked, throwing the carton at him which his friend deflected with his arm onto the floor as a tiny dreg of light pink spilled out onto the floor.

The dress was extremely soft but also breathable and matched her tone. Autumn felt overwhelming joy but also immense gratitude towards Taeyang. She decided to check herself out properly in the bathroom mirror since the reaction she had received was so positive. Yet there was something bothering her. It was a nice gesture. But it was too generous. It made her feel guilty and confused. "Why did he do this?" she asked herself as she touched the sides of her dress. "Did he really feel that bad about losing her manuscript? Or did he just hate her clothes?" "What if he...?" she questioned internally before shaking her head. He was just a jerk. One who had a nice side. That's it. Her mind felt confused by the whole thing. Autumn had never been in this type of situation before. Her hands were restless, the gravity of the situation seeping into her anxieties like a weight within her chest.

Hyeon casually scuttled by Autumn as she made her way back into the living room. Taeyang sat on the edge of the couch reading, his posture was awfully relaxed for someone who was so uptight. She abruptly coughed; but he didn't move a muscle. She whistled, causing Taeyang to give her the side-eye. "He's being a jerk again. Go figure," she concluded in her mind. But in reality, Taeyang was trying to keep his mind under control. She resembled a model, the way she was standing there with her hair pushed back behind her left ear. Now that she was completely rejuvenated, she had become a completely different woman, and he did his best to stop his mouth from gaping open right there and then as he got a proper look at her. The book within his fingers slipped from his fingers to the spot next to him.

He rubbed his legs with his hands trying to formulate his words carefully.

She remained there - feeling shy at his silence. At any moment she expected a sarcastic remark, a snicker, or something along the lines of 'There are windows that could wear it better,' but she was met with resounding silence. Not only that, but the book he'd been enjoying was at his side, completely forgotten.

Autumn cleared her throat hoping this would rouse him, but he seemed completely spaced out. His eyes had a dazed look about them. Autumn opened her mouth but stopped, she wanted to tell him that although the gesture was incredibly considerate she could not accept it.

"The dress suits you. Is it comfortable?" he asked her, breaking the silence.

"Yeah, it is. Thank you. But this is too much. It's too generous," she said, gratitude mixed with guilt beamed from her smiling face.

He waved it off. "It's all good, I'm not a broke bum you know, I can afford whatever I want," Taeyang bragged.

She raised a brow at his uncouth tongue that had a tendency to run wild. Before she tried again, however, he held up his hand and she could not protest further.

He stood up and grabbed Autumn's hand pulling her aside.

"Autumn stop worrying, it's fine," he insisted.

Autumn opened her mouth to speak again until Taeyang held her jaw with the edge of his fingers inching closer to her face.

"Don't ruin my good mood. It's rare that I'm in one and since I am, this is your first and only warning. It is fine, your clothes were ugly. Now you have nicer ones, so stop," he said before letting her go.

Autumn huffed before stepping back. She was annoyed at his constant digs in regard to her taste in fashion but she couldn't fight the blush that crawled across her cheeks at their proximity. It didn't help that his fingertips left a mark on her tanned skin.

She nodded in defeat whilst avoiding his gaze. Taeyang smirked and patted her head to her dismay. "I'm not a dog," she thought to herself, tempted to slap his hand away. Hyeon coughed causing the two to jump back from each other. Autumn waved at him a little too quickly with a sugary smile suddenly adorning her face, as Taeyang twitched his hands and didn't meet his gaze. He looked about at the peach wallpaper of the living room which suddenly became a point of interest for him. Hyeon smirked cheekily as he lifted his eyebrows suggestively before winking at Taeyang who mouthed something unintelligible at him. Autumn decided at that point that the black scuff on the floor was the most interesting thing in the world.

"It's not what you think, Hyeon. Don't start," Taeyang warned in Korean before pushing past him.

Hyeon mimicked him in a high-pitched tone before grinning at Autumn who coughed before leaving.

Taeyang sat in their dorm room feeling frustrated. The company had called an emergency meeting. Since there were rumours going around about the boys having a mysterious woman in their dorm. It was on the news also. He really didn't need any of this right now.

Soon Woo chewed on a piece of mint gum, his leg shaking, as he sat there waiting. He couldn't have his phone, the risk of having it confiscated was too high. What it made it worse was that he had a particularly cute booty call waiting for him. He scowled, looking around, as he tried to spot an opening in which he could bolt. He loved being an idol, but he hated it when his responsibilities interfered with his private activities. He rubbed his legs in slow back and forth motions; he was certain that if he became any more tense, he would have a heart attack. He cast his gaze to Taeyang, who from what he could see, was formulating some sort of a plan. The way his face tensed before contracting. They locked eyes. An understanding passed between them.

Taeyang sat there messing with his ring. He hated meetings. It always felt like an excuse for the company to complain about something. Kim filled out his sudoku book whilst Hyeon played with a lilac rubber ball as the others talked amongst themselves. They had been there for a while. But it was clear that trouble was brewing. The potential punishments they could have dished out to them today over these rumours was the worst part of this meeting. The receptionist kept rushing back and forth to her desk looking unsettled and very anxious. The bosses made the staff do the most menial tasks just to flex their authority.

An older official looking man walked towards them looking at them with what seemed to be a mixture of compassion and scrutiny.

"It's time to face the music, boys," he said before leading them into the metallic brown lift.

They bowed as they entered the room. The CEOs looked notably displeased. Chen arranged them into a singular line starting with Taeyang since he was their leader. The boardroom was on the top floor of the building. The room had a wide flat screen TV which was turned off, an elongated oak table with slim beige leather seated chairs. The windows behind the boys were huge, giving a clear view of Seoul.

The floor was a swirly white and black marble that glistened under the light. Their shoes tapped against it when they moved. The silence from their bosses in the room was deafening.

Taeyang bit down on his tongue, he knew that if they started an argument today, it would not end well for any of them. Their new album was set to come out in a few weeks. Knowing the company, it was possible that they would scrap it completely if these rumours were confirmed to be true. The oldest CEO, Mr Quay, stood, staring each member down. Judgement, condescension, and above all else disappointment was projected onto each of them.

"Is it true? You boys are holding a woman in your dorm? Is she a prostitute?" he asked them.

"No sir. These are baseless rumours started by netizens," Taeyang spoke, trying to keep his cool.

Not appreciating the insinuation that Autumn was such a thing.

Mr Quay eyed him for a moment before turning his attention to Kim.

"Hm, well, I know you wouldn't do anything like that Taeyang. But not all of your members are as...controlled," he spoke, staring at Kim as he did.

This hit a nerve with Kim who was already angry about the idea that Autumn was some kind of sex worker.

"With that said, you have failed in your duties as their leader. It is your job to keep them in line. In this regard you are nothing but a failure," Mr Quay remarked.

Taeyang was about to speak when Kim did something that shocked them all.

Kim went forward and slapped Mr Quay, his rage souring as skin connected. Taeyang had done nothing but protect their group, motivate them and help them sail through the roughest years pre-debut. To even suggest that he was a failure was insulting to them all.

Taeyang grabbed his arm pulling it back trying to intervene but Kim pushed him back seeing red. His repressed hatred for Mr Quay spilling out as he went in for another go but their manager, Chen yanked his wrist back with such force that his shoulder clicked.

"That's enough Kim! Do you want to be fired?!" the older man yelled at him holding him back.

Soon Woo stood there, mouth gaping as a smile lit up on his face, if Kim hadn't smacked him, then he would have done. That asshole was begging for it. He had been on their case for a while and insulting Taeyang like that was crossing the line. Snapping from his spell he joined Kim's side helping to restrain him. As Taeyang bowed apologetically.

Mr Quay rubbed his face, his expression darkening before sitting back at the table.

"You're all dismissed but Kim. Also, Taeyang consider your next salary – deducted. Maybe that will motivate you to do a better job." he seethed before dismissing them with a hand.

Taeyang stood to his full height and glared at Kim who was shooting daggers at Mr Quay. "Great, just what I needed today," Taeyang thought, angry at his friend's misguided actions. Chen smacked the back of Kim's head before pushing him down to bow with his hand. He protested under his breath; this went unheeded by his manager who wanted to skin the daylights out of him. The boys were ushered out by the official man from earlier who gave each of them a death glare. "Stupid brats," he thought.

Autumn waited for any sign of the boys. She checked her phone but there were no new texts. She took a deep breath placing her phone onto the table, she tried repeating Taeyang's words inside of her mind.

"I'm too valuable to be fired. Don't worry, leafy," he had said it so confidently.

But she wasn't certain. She sipped on her caramel latte, glancing at the front door from time to time. The bell above the door jingled but it was just an older woman coming in.

Autumn stood up as she saw Taeyang enter with a large hoodie on and a pair of sunglasses covering his face. There was no smirk, no sarcastic comment, he just walked towards her.

Taeyang bowed so Autumn returned the gesture. He caught her off guard when he gave her a hug. Autumn slowly enveloped Taeyang, his silence was deafening. The meeting must have been an absolute disaster for him to be acting so shaken. Taeyang, on the other hand, didn't know why but he just needed a hug. Dealing with his boss had been stressful and he just needed relief. Autumn stroked his back gently before he pushed her away and sat down opting to steal her coffee. Hyeon caught up with them, panting as he tried to speak.

"Where is Kim?" Autumn pried.

Taeyang remained quiet, sipping on his coffee.

Hyeon on the other hand spoke up.

"Still with our CEO."

Autumn picked at her nail.

"Is he okay?" she tried again

"No, he smacked the CEO. So, he is probably going to be kicked out of the group," Hyeon said sadly.

"Why did he smack him?" Autumn asked causing Taeyang to smack the table.

"It doesn't matter! What he did was idiotic and now we are all in hot water!" he snapped.

"Taeyang, are you okay?" Autumn asked, taken aback by his anger.

"No. I'm not. I'm going to kick that idiot's behind for this!" he spat before storming off.

Autumn was shocked. She knew it had been bad but seeing him this upset bothered her. She got up and followed him failing to hear Hyeon who called after her. All she cared about was finding Taeyang before he got into more trouble. She chased after Taeyang, pushing past crowds of random people as her heart pounded. She was afraid that he would do something further to provoke his boss's wrath. She couldn't have that. Autumn spotted his black hoodie in the distance and pushed her legs harder until she went by a side street. A tanned arm leapt out from the darkness and grabbed her waist, Autumn tried to scream but a large, calloused hand came over her mouth reeking of boot polish. Autumn tried to claw and kick at her captors, but it was no use. She felt a sharp prick in her neck before the world dissolved into nothingness.

Taeyang climbed up the plastic ladder onto the roof. Kim hadn't been at the company building. So, he came up here to cool down. He perched himself on a rusty air vent, the fury he had felt earlier simmered down into guilt along with shame biting at his heels. Kim was trying to defend him which was nice but in doing so he made his life harder. He held his head wishing that Kim was here with a packet of cigarettes or at least some strong alcohol. Most of the time he hated the cigarettes especially; they make your teeth yellow and make your voice harsh. But his stress levels were making him want to scream. He didn't notice Hyeon who was approaching him in a panicked state.

Hyeon panted, "I-it's...A-autumn!" he gasped as he hunched over.

This caught Taeyang's attention who whipped his head around so quickly that it clicked as he did.

Taeyang left up and grabbed Hyeon's collar. His own turmoil forgotten.

"What about her?!" Taeyang hissed, tightening his hold. Hyeon squirmed,

"She's been taken!" he blurted out, panic dancing in his eyes.

Taeyang's face was becoming thirty different shades of blistering red the more he heard.

"T-they were wearing black, and then they just vanished. I didn't know what to do." Hyeon continued on trying to hold on to the tiny amount of air he could get in this position.

Taeyang's heart stopped at that, Autumn had been taken because he left without thinking.

"It's not your fault. But I need to get her back before she is harmed," Taeyang responded, barely repressing his rage.

Hyeon yanked his arm back before he could go. "Taeyang! You can't just go after her. You don't know where she was taken!" he chastised.

Taeyang shoved off his hand.

"I have to get her back! What do you suggest, I leave her?" he yelled.

Hyeon sweated profusely, feeling the weight of Taeyang's glare boring into his jade hues.

"N-no but-" Hyeon started but was cut off.

"Come or don't, but don't get in my way," he warned.

"I-I won't. The last time I saw her she was two streets away from the café," he explained, rubbing his sore neck.

Taeyang nodded before running off. Hyeon trailing behind.

"I promise you Autumn, I will find you," Taeyang vowed to himself.

Machines screeching, and hammering were the first things Autumn heard as she woke up from her hasty slumber. There was a stone pillar pressed against her back. A dark cloth covered her eyes, and she could feel rope binding her wrists as well as a sting in her neck a gag in her mouth. Her heart pulsed inside of her ears, the gravelly concrete beneath her legs grated against her sensitive skin. She had sweat beading down her face, terror started to rise within her at the thought of the Sasaengs kidnapping her. Her stomach clenched, and twisted, and the adrenaline she felt gave her jitters. There was a dripping echoing somewhere behind her. The ground was unforgiving and heartless to her behind.

Footsteps echoed getting closer until they came to a stop. A man cleared his throat before addressing her. "Ah, it seems our little sleeping hostage is awake,"

Autumn mumbled something in return but the restraint on her mouth made it unclear.

The man ripped off the restraint and kneeled down.

"Can you repeat that, sweet cheeks?" he whispered harshly.

She quivered; the gravelly voice of the man put her on edge. His English had an American twang to it. It felt kind of put on. But she was too scared to psychoanalyse him at the moment.

"Who are you?" she snapped as heart hammered away.

The men chortled; this kindled her stress and anger which was skyrocketing further with each second in their company.

"I am Damien and my associate is called Chris, we are friends of that Taeyang fella you've been trailing after," he whispered, invading her personal space more with each word.

She sneered at him. "What about him?"

"He owes us money. A lot of money. You are the collateral. If he doesn't pay up then we take you as payment. Now, I don't want to hurt you but we are going to get that money. One way or another," Damien said before grabbing her chin.

His fingers felt rough and unkempt. He wafted generic peppermint all around her as he talked which made her want to gag. Although she couldn't see their faces, she had a hunch that they were just as cheap and nasty looking as they smelt and acted.

Autumn refused to believe it. Taeyang would never do such a thing to her. As arrogant and anti-social as he could be, he wasn't a malicious person. His vibrant smile, the twinkle of his Mallen streak. The way his brown eyes swirled into a million shades when he was joyful, and the care along with the thought he put into the things he did for people. That wasn't someone who was capable of this kind of thing.

"I wish he was here," she whispered to herself shedding a few tears.

The man smirked, letting go of her jaw. Satisfied with her pain.

"You never know, there might be other uses for a woman as cute as you," Damien taunted before twirling a loose strand of her hair.

This made her feel violated and her tears vanished as she boiled with anger. She had to do something to defend herself.

Autumn turned her cheek and bit his finger hard until she drew blood. He slapped her and was about to drag her up when his partner yanked his suit collar hard.

"Look dude, if we damage her then there will be no negotiating anything," Chris reminded him.

Taeyang scoured around the area for Autumn asking people if they had seen anything before a frenzy of fans spotted him through his disguise and screwed up the search. Now, Taeyang was joined by the rest of the group who were gathered in the dorm with their perturbed manager. The paparazzi were all over the place but there were hired security guards outside keeping them in. Chen walked off to the kitchen smacking Taeyang's head in the process. Taeyang made a mental note to get him back for that later. The rumours were escalating so their company ordered an emergency press conference. Dark Star Seven were escorted from their dorm to a news building where the conference was being held.

Taeyang's phone was constantly beeping with calls from sasaengs, news outlets, colleagues and other fans but not one single text from Autumn. He cursed under his breath staring into his lap. Worry entrapped his heart shaking it to the core. His eyes darted between his manager and bandmates. He cooked up an idea whilst he continued stewing in what felt like the worst plastic seat in the world.

After two hours the press conference finally concluded, Taeyang bowed at a 90-degree angle before leaving. He was in no mood to sign autographs or exchange any kind of pleasantries with anyone. He wiped the sweat along with the caked-on make-up from his brow trying to cool down. The media and fans had bought the excuse about the entire charade being a stunt for their new album. In the wake of their press release, pre-orders for their album tripled with the story making it into the international headlines. For this reason, the CEOs chose not to scrap their upcoming album but there were stricter rules the boys now had to follow as a result. One of which was, no fraternising outside of the group or management. He figured that his management would go this route. They seemed to get off on being controlling.

Taeyang formulated a plan for this, he couldn't just abandon Autumn especially knowing that she was stuck somewhere with God only knows who. He needed Hyeon to come with him, they couldn't all go since it would create suspicion. He excused himself to go to the bathroom. Chen trailed behind him until he stepped inside. Taeyang pulled out his phone and texted the group his plan before flushing the toilet. Then he turned on the tap for a minute before giving himself a once over in the mirror. He smirked, admiring his perfectly shaped jaw. He left the bathroom giving Chen a smirk who glared back before he was dragged back into the living room.

Autumn's heart galloped; her confidence faltered as she heard whispering in the dark. "Please let this be a stupid nightmare," she pleaded repeatedly within the depths of her mind. Her hands were stinging from the rough material of the restraints. She tried twisting her wrists to give herself enough space to at least feel less restricted. She managed to loosen the rope a bit but not enough to completely unstrap her hands. Her hands touched the rough ground. A wave of relief washed over her as the pain left her wrists. Now the main discomfort she was experiencing came from her legs that had started to cramp and lose all feeling.

Her mind drifted to Taeyang again, his smile, that particularly confident one laced with a million secrets, and words that were left unknown. The way he could eat piles of food and not gain a single pound. How he sprayed his cologne from right to left because he believed it made the scent last longer. Or how he pretended to know every fact and topic under the sun just because he read a book on it. She smirked a little, he could be such an asshole but she liked it.

"There is no way he did what they are accusing him of. I just know it. There has to be something else at play here." Autumn thought as she continued to try and free herself.

She felt a lighter set of shoes vibrating on the concrete floor. Her body stilled, but the closer the individual got the calmer she started to feel as soon as she smelt a familiar aftershave. Autumn could've jumped for joy right there and then. Two soft and firm hands touched her head as the blindfold started to slip off from her face revealing who she had suspected all along; Taeyang. Her eyes squinted as the light made them ache. But she couldn't fight the relieved smile forming on her face. He had found her.

"Are you okay?" he whispered as he got to work at setting her hands free from the ropes.

"U-uh yeah just shaken and a little bruised," she admitted as her voice quivered.

Taeyang could see the terror in her eyes.

"Well, well, well, looky what we have here? The idol prince decided to grace us with his presence," Damien interrupted as he and Chris emerged.

Taeyang glared at Damien who was holding a knife.

"Step back or she'll be harmed," Damien warned.

Taeyang stepped back not wanting to risk her safety.

"Dammit! Where are you Hyeon?" he thought to himself.

The duo looked at each other before chuckling.

"Listen, flower boy. We want our moolah," he sneered.

"What money?" Taeyang asked looking between Autumn and the two.

"The money your manager borrowed for your latest promotion. He said that you set this deal up, if the moolah wasn't repaid then we'd take cutie pie here as collateral," Damien explained.

"I don't know what you are talking about. If anyone is behind this, it's that bastard, Chen. I had nothing to do with it," Taeyang seethed, upon hearing this new information.

"Either way. Give us the goods or she dies," Damien replied before smirking.

"Nah, I have a better idea," Taeyang said, before approaching them.

"To hell with waiting. If I do, she might die," he thought fearfully to himself.

Both Damien and Chris looked at him as if he was nuts. He was by himself without a weapon. What was he going to do? Sing them a pretty little song?

As she watched this interaction Autumn wanted to scream, tell him to run but her throat was too dry to utter a sound. Taeyang smirked at Damien wagging his finger. She knew that fire in his brown eyes, the same one that made its presence known only when he was on the edge of blowing up. Her body tingled in its presence. Taeyang was a multitude of things but a coward was not one of them. She needed a plan, and fast. These men were going to kill him if something didn't give and soon.

Damien placed the knife against her head. Despite her fear, Autumn winked at Taeyang. Then she elbowed the man's face, knocking the knife out of his hand. it slid across the floor before Hyeon ran in and grabbed it.

"It's about time!" Taeyang snapped in Korean at Hyeon before rushing towards Autumn only to be tackled by Damien.

Taeyang wrestled with Damien. Hyeon stood there frozen. Violence frightened him a great deal. Chris lunged at Taeyang who dodged him before delivering one forceful blow to Damien's face. Knocking him out cold.

Hyeon tossed the knife away not knowing what to do as Chris then lunged at him. Hyeon kicked him and punched him as Chris tried to knock him to the ground. But Hyeon twisted his body around, causing Chris to fall. Taeyang intervened stamping the man in the nuts before delivering a punch across his face. Hyeon was astonished and relieved because he really hated fighting. Taeyeon tossed the bodies next to the pillar that Autumn had been tied to, and stuck his tongue out at them before he walked away.

Taeyang checked over Autumn who looked absolutely exhausted and he helped her up removing the rest of the rope. Her face was a medley of emotion and her eyes were puffy and crusted from crying so much.

Autumn smacked his chest gently, her face was puffy, and raw but to Taeyang seeing her standing there relatively unharmed aside from the bruise on her face was all that he cared about. Hyeon saw the exchange opting to give them a moment in private as he walked off. The men were slumped on the floor unconscious, as blood pooled beneath them. Police sirens blared in the distance so Taeyang grabbed Autumn's hand, and sprinted towards the exit side door. Relieved that he was able to save her.

Once they were outside, and a good distance away from the building, Taeyang pulled Autumn to the side of the road to inspect her for any other injuries. He noticed splotches of blood on her dress. Taeyang checked her hands, and discovered where the blood had been coming from. The hand she had used to knock the knife away had a sharp cut across the top. The wound wasn't deep enough to need stitches but would still take a few days to heal. Taeyang ripped a piece of his sandstone sweatshirt off and bandaged Autumn's hand with it. She averted her eyes, thoughts swirled in her mind. On one hand, she was relieved that Taeyang and Hyeon were in one piece yet she was furious. If Taeyang had just given her the manuscript in the first place then none of this would have happened. She stepped away from him before smacking his chest. Autumn smacked it again, and again, and again before he restrained her wrists. Shock overtaking her.

Taeyang was annoyed at the first hit. But when he saw her eyes, the chaos swirling behind her sea orbs, he understood that she was overwhelmed. He held her letting her vent her frustrations through violent sobs that erupted from her. Hyeon came back with three cups of iced coffee, and a bar of chocolate for each of them. He felt alarmed at her distressed state but one smile from Taeyang alleviated his concern slightly. He rubbed her back, letting her work through it. After a few minutes she calmed down enough to speak to them.

"T-thanks g-guys, I'm sorry for frightening you both," she said rubbing her eyes.

They sat on a bench in silence with Autumn refusing to let go of Taeyang's hand. Under normal circumstances he would have ripped his hand away but given what had just transpired he decided to let it lie. Hyeon kept looking over at her to ensure that she really was okay. Taeyang finished his chocolate bar before stuffing the wrapper into his pocket. Autumn hadn't touched hers, opting to guzzle down her coffee instead. They sat in silence for a while until Hyeon got up to take and dispose of their empty wrappers and drinks.

When Hyeon came back, Autumn was dozing off, barely keeping her head up, and it dawned on Taeyang how late it was getting. Due to the attention that was on them, he couldn't take her back to the dorm. He decided to call a few people who owed him a favour whilst Hyeon watched her. Hyeon sat next to Autumn, he took off his coat and wrapped it around her shoulders. The temperature was becoming chilly, and her dress wasn't suited for this kind of weather. Hyeon couldn't deny however, the relief he felt that Autumn was basically unharmed aside from some cuts and bruises. He hummed softly as he watched her sleeping form, her eyes fully closed at this point.

Taeyang returned after thirty minutes with some news.

"Kim called, he managed to cover for us, but we don't have tons of time. I'm going to a friend's place with Autumn, you head back to the dorm," he ordered before scooping Autumn into his arms.

"Okay boss," Hyeon responded before leaving.

Exhaustion clawed behind his eyes; his knees buckled weakly as his ankle moaned but he kept going. They both needed a place to rest and recover, in the morning they would search for the manuscript and help Autumn get home in time. But for now, she needed rest and so did he. Taeyang held her close as he picked up the pace, he had failed himself, he had almost failed his band, but he would not fail her no matter what happens. Seeing her hurt today, created an ache in his soul. One he didn't understand but also one he didn't want to feel again.

Hyeon snuck into the dorm, meeting Kim who was taking quick drags on a half-smoked cigarette as he sat at the window.

"She, okay?" Kim asked.

"She's okay. Taeyang has her," he said as Kim stubbed out his cigarette.

"Good. It'd be a shame to see such a pretty girl die for a bum like our precious leader," he remarked to Hyeon before leaving the room.

He was furious with Taeyang for not standing up for him earlier and upon learning that he went back to the company building to kiss his ass.

Soon Woo spoke up.

"Ignore him, he's just upset because the CEO gave him a beating. Although Mr Quay deserved the hit. He should know better than to pull that stuff with our bosses,"

The boys gave each other a knowing look.

Hours had passed with no word from Taeyang. Kim sighed, checking his phone, there were no new messages from him. He could hear Chen's rough voice echoing from the stairway. Hyeon scrambled toward his bed pulling his cute little plushie under the covers with him. Kim laughed at his friend, "Really? You still sleep with that ridiculous thing?" he asked but received an embarrassed mumble in response.

He rushed into his own bed, smirking, before the door opened.

Chen had left an hour ago. The boys were locked in their dorm with two security personnel patrolling the perimeter, his services were no longer required for the night. He had checked their bedroom making sure the boys were asleep. The guards had been given strict orders to punish the boys however they see fit if they broke the rules and left the dorm. "Idiots," he thought as he left the building. Putting aside the fact that he was almost fired by the CEOs today. The boys had come scathingly close to a damaging scandal that would have tanked their careers and caused him financial issues. He slammed the white car door shut resting his head against the leather steering wheel for a minute before driving off.

Taeyang placed Autumn on the guest bed of his friend, Heechul's house. She hadn't woken up once during their taxi ride here. So, he swapped out his grubby makeshift bandage for a proper one. She looked so delicate lying on the black sheets, she whimpered, twitching in her sleep. He stroked her head softly feeling guilty. "I never should have left that café. I was just so angry at him, Autumn," he thought to himself as he looked at her.

"I promise I will get your manuscript back this time," he gently vowed before covering her over with a sheer cotton blanket.

Taeyang sat at the bottom of the bed. His thoughts were bothersome. Initially he was worried that they could have been followed by sasaengs but he quickly dismissed that thought, even the wackiest ones wouldn't travel this far just to find him. After all, he was on the other side of Seoul. His friend, Heechul, worked as an IT executive and preferred to live closer to the peaceful wilderness than the bustling city. The house resembled a Hanok (a traditional Korean style house) but had a couple of extra rooms. There was a cold tingling coming over his neck that was eerily similar to what he felt before, but he dismissed it since there was no way that a sasaeng followed him here.

Taeyang sauntered into the bathroom to freshen up. He took a good and hard look in the small yet clean mirror, his porcelain skin was dull and a little greasy but what made him scowl considerably was when he noticed a few ugly blackheads forming on his t-zone. Taeyang had been so distracted with everything that had been going that he had neglected his eight-step skincare routine. "This won't do," he thought to himself as he pulled out his friend's face cleanser from the basket pumping a couple of clear drops onto his palm. By the time Taeyang left the bathroom his porcelain face was spotless, and he felt completely renewed. His appearance wasn't everything to him, but it was important for his job and image.

Upon entering the living room, he found Heechul sitting on the couch eating a bowl of steamed white rice, and sticky tofu. Taeyang played with his friend's fluffy bleached hair before plopping down next to him. Heechul brushed him off, stabbing a chopstick into a piece of tofu before chewing a bit. Taeyang watched the TV. The news was boring, but one story did pique his interest. Two men were in critical condition in hospital after being found at the industrial parking complexes. Taeyang snickered at that - feeling proud of himself, the report went on to state that the men were wanted on theft, and human trafficking charges. The last part made him sit up.

"How did Chen know them and why did he use Autumn? How did he know?" he thought to himself.

Heechul stopped eating, he flicked Taeyang's ear trying to lighten the heavy expression on his friend's face. Which caused him to glare at Heechul who yanked the remote from his friend's hand. The news was boring plus there was a new episode airing tonight of a k-drama that he was currently overly invested in.

The next day...

Taeyang wanted to scope out this location before taking Autumn along, but he needed to stop by the dorm first which he managed to do but only just. For what exactly? He never specified but it was most likely something to do with his other plans. He also instructed that Heechul had to kindly give her the rundown once she was out of bed. He didn't know much about Autumn, but from what Taeyang had told him, it seemed like she would not approve of this plan.

Chen checked Taeyang's temperature, the inside of his mouth and his nose before roughly dropping him back onto the bed. Taeyang scrunched up his face when Chen turned his back. His methods for ensuring that they were obeying orders were strange to say the least. Hyeon laughed but turned it into a cough when his stoic manager raised a brow at him. The room was checked over and it went well until Chen found an opened condom packet in the desk drawer. Taeyang stifled a laugh knowing exactly who it belonged to but was elbowed back into the bed by Hyeon who looked disgusted. Their manager inspected the item thoroughly. "You think he'd be familiar with these by now," Taeyang scoffed in his mind before Chen placed the offensive item into his coat pocket. After a thorough scolding from Chen, Taeyang decided to wait around for a little bit before leaving.

"Time for next stage," Taeyang remarked confidently.

He stripped out of his PJ's and into a pair of dark blue jeans with a lime sweatshirt and black baseball cap. He fixed his ink blue locks in the mirror making sure that no hair was out of place. Taking a second, he composed himself. His nerves were in high gear today, but knowing what his friends were about to do for him brightened his spirit. Getting into the dorm had been a risk, one that he knew he had to do differently upon leaving.

Since they couldn't do much without being noticed Hyeon and Taemin agreed to pretend to be women to distract the crowd and security long enough for Taeyang to leave.

Two rather tall and lanky people wearing ugly floral dresses sprung out from the bushes in front of the building. Hyeon speed walked out of area clutching his sister's old purse whilst Taemin distracted the crowd by pretending to have stolen one of Taeyang's socks. The security guards noticed Hyeon and started to chase him. So, he sped up and ducked past the crowd as fans rushed over in drips breaking the trail. Security tried to grab Taemin. This ticked off the fans who were fawning over him because he managed to get so close to the band. They scuffled with the guards who were calling for reinforcements; more fans gathered.

Within a few minutes Dark Star Seven fans were duking it out with the security guards. Taeyang grinned before advancing into the bathroom. "That should hold them off for a while," he articulated to himself. Taeyang jumped out of the bathroom window. The distance was a few feet so nothing bone shattering if he fell plus his ankle had been healing so the risk of injury was low in his estimation. Taeyang dusted himself off before he dashed off.

Autumn scrubbed the dishes clanking them loudly, Heechul went to the fridge grabbing his lunchbox. Her hand stung, the pain had woken her up, and on top of the nightmare she endured last night she was informed about Taeyang's crazy plan to get her manuscript back which irritated her further. She wiped another plate placing it into the drying rack.

"Um, I'm going to work. You okay here?" Heechul asked looking at her cautiously.

She gave a small nod before washing the remaining soiled dishes. Heechul waved goodbye before turning to leave.

"Wait!" Autumn blurted out as she remembered something.

He looked at her curiously as she removed the yellow washing up gloves from her hands, placing them on the side of the sink.

"Thanks, for helping us out last night," she told him before she bowed at a 45-degree angle.

He was taken aback by the gesture but returned her bow, a prominent blush spread rapidly across his cheeks making them warm.

Taeyang hid in thick white rose bushes. Thorns poked his behind whilst small brown twigs prodded his sides, but he ignored it with only one objective in mind. He pulled out a set of green binoculars from his pocket. The occupants inside of the building were shuffling about upstairs. He hated waiting, but Autumn's career depended on it, and he just couldn't let her down. The eldest girl in the house was out of focus – according to his informant she was the mastermind behind this whole situation. But the younger one appeared to be leaving the building.

After both of them had left Taeyang made sure the coast was clear as he peered over the bush once again making sure that the girls were out of sight. Once twenty minutes had gone by without either of the girls returning for anything, Taeyang checked the notes his informant had sent him, before going up to the house. He hoped that the manuscript was still together and not torn or defaced with obscurity by these unhinged bitches. The sight of Autumn's broken heart was not something he wanted to bear witness to at all. He shook his head trying to shrug off the thought, then again, it could go the other way. Maybe seeing her manuscript screwed up would cause her to go into an intolerable rage where she would rip the faces off the girls before using them as a purse. He laughed at how ridiculous that would be, but he had to admit that he found her attempts at being angry quite cute.

Autumn had cleaned the kitchen and was in the process of vacuuming the living room when Taeyang entered - his vibe seemed lighter.

The noise of the machine drowned out the door. "I can't believe that he would do that. He's either crazy or stupid," she recalled thinking about what Heechul had told her when she got up.

Taeyang smirked and unplugged the plug from the wall socket. The shriek died instantly; Autumn pushed the vacuum, rattling it, before she looked to Taeyang. Who stood there, swinging the plug in his hand.

If looks could slam someone repeatedly into a wall until they were begging for mercy, hers certainly would in this moment.

He grinned, folding his arms, "I think turning it on would help, Autumn," he remarked.

She shot daggers at him before clearing her throat.

"And just when did you become the authority on vacuum cleaners, smartass?" she spat with playfulness underlining her agitated tone.

Wagging his finger, he retorted, "Uh-uh now, that's not how we say thank you."

She stood there, irritated, as her playfulness slipped away.

"For what? For you almost exposing yourself?" she snapped.

His eyes narrowed as a glint of mystery danced around his hazel swirls. He ignored her attempt to change the subject.

"So what? Are you the queen of vacuums now?"

She rolled her eyes at him. "For your information, Mr Smartass, I'm not and unlike SOME people I know HOW to use a vacuum because unlike CERTAIN people I don't have everyone else doing MY bidding," she roasted back.

His eyebrow twitched at this, his face becoming pink as his lips stretched back until they were white. Her comment actually annoyed him.

"Is that so? Well, unlike certain feeble, whiny, curtain wearing, cry-baby nyeo-" he was cut off from his string of insults by her hand hitting his face.

When had she gotten so close to him? Maybe he didn't notice but it was like she glided across the floor at times.

Taeyang wanted to be angry. So angry. But something about her skin against his made him feel magical, a shiver shot through his body, lighting a fire in his lower half. The pain stung at his cheek, to hell with pissing her off, he wanted her body at this point. If she had this much fire in her words, God only knows what the fire is like in her-

His moment of introspection was cut off by Autumn's anger.

"Well, if CERTAIN people aren't careful then THEY are going to be finding their VALUABLES at the end of this vacuum!" she retorted, holding up the vacuum's tip.

Taeyang scoffed, grinning at her.

"I bet you'd love MY VALUABLES at the edge of your vacuum!" he shot back thoughtlessly.

"NOT. IN. YOUR. DREAMS! PERVERT!" she retorted.

Autumn prodded his chest with the vacuum tip exemplifying every syllable, resisting the temptation to give him a vasectomy with her tongue. He had gone off and risked his reputation, as well as his wellbeing to retrieve her manuscript. The gesture was nice but the way he went about it angered her no end. It was reckless. Those sasaengs could have been waiting for him and harmed him. She wanted him to feel her anger.

Taeyang knocked the vacuum tip out of her hands as he annoyed her further. Their stare locked, as they challenged each other to cross the line. To break the silence, but Taeyang's hunger was rising as his tolerance was sinking. He wanted to bend her over the table and - he stopped his mind. "What the hell am I thinking?" he thought to himself. As his phone vibrated, he was reminded of something important.

"Whatever Autumn. Oh, and call your dumb agent before you are fired," he said to her pushing his phone into her chest.

He left to go take a cold shower. He really needed one after this escapade.

Autumn held his phone before marching down the hallway to call her agent. She was expecting the ear-bashing of a lifetime for going quiet on her, but she didn't care about that at this point. The deadline loomed over her head, and she didn't want to let her fans, agent or her publisher down. She contemplated just running off without saying anything to that temperamental dumbass. The mixed signals he was giving were hurting her more than she wanted to let on.

Chapter Four

Page Turner Worth Of Problems

The house surprised Autumn. It was aesthetically pleasing on the outside. A type of cottage you would see in a landscape painting surrounded by a little evergreen forest. Autumn yelped as a sharp thorn poked her behind. Taeyang quickly covered her mouth pushing her forward. According to Taeyang her manuscript was somewhere inside of this house.

"Don't be loud, yelling isn't common here and you might blow our cover," he whispered.

"But you... the other day..." she retorted, nudging his shoulder with her own.

He hunched his shoulders, rolling his eyes.

"I was upset, but still, it's not common to yell in South Korea. Honestly, I thought Canadians were quiet, and jovial people until I met you," he baited her.

"Har har very funny hoser," she replied before kicking a chipped stone into a murky puddle wishing that it was his balls instead.

"Are you coming? I know that my chiselled body is irresistible to look at but pick a better time and place," he quipped before approaching the house.

She clenched her teeth. Taeyang didn't miss the blush blotching across her cheeks. His stare lingered for a few seconds before he closed the gap between himself and the door.

Taeyang carefully pushed the door open. These sasaengs never locked it which struck him as odd but they didn't seem that bright to begin with. Autumn hovered behind him; the smell that greeted them made her heart sink. Between grimy dumpsters, creepy men, and old takeout, her nose was becoming numb and resentful. He removed his shoes, and signalled her to do the same. She sighed, removing her brown wedges. The living room was bare; only a TV, a spider plant, and a wooden chair decorated the room along with magazines scattered here and there. He checked his phone, according to the info he was given they would gone for two hours. "Stalking my dorm presumably," he moaned inside of his mind before stuffing his hands in his pockets.

They travelled further into the house. In the hallway there were cut out pictures of the boys plastered on each wall with fresh pink lipstick stains smearing them. Autumn had dealt with her own obsessive fan experience but nothing on this level – this was creepy and somewhat cringy. She was broken from her thoughts when Taeyang sneezed. She gave him a judgemental look when he pulled out a white silk handkerchief before wiping his nose. He rolled his eyes at her before flicking her with the handkerchief. This caused her to scrunch her face up as she batted it away with her hand. "It's just too easy," he thought to himself upon seeing her all frustrated and nervous.

Taeyang stepped over some dirty clothes, there was a stout coffee table with scratches across it. The room felt stuffy with a musty smell polluting the air. Autumn pinched her nose; the smell made the insides of her nose itch. Taeyang couldn't see anything that resembled a box in here, so he continued on. The house had a strange vibe to it in the way that the furniture was placed and the fact that there were no lightbulbs in the sockets.

"How do people live here, eh? It's as if the place has been gutted of its soul," she made note of her observations aloud as they continued.

"Saesangs don't have souls. Just delusions," Taeyang replied as he looked around.

They made their way up the wooden stairway, then followed that by entering what seemed to be one of the bedrooms. Taeyang entered first, he scanned the area before signalling Autumn to follow him. Taeyang made his way into the bedroom. What he saw in this room lit the flames of fury inside of his bloodshot chocolate eyes. Autumn's eyes welled up as she clutched her heart, there were pictures of her on the walls that were defiled with the eyes cut out. Not being able to bear the sight, she turned to leave but Taeyang wrapped her hand around his own. He knew that feeling. He felt the same way the first time something like this happened to him. Seeing her so hurt made him want to protect her. So, he chose to grab her hand.

Autumn's stress dropped; the warmth of his skin mingled with her own causing her muscles to unclench. Her horror dimmed as she processed the situation rationally. It was only pictures; they were just crazy people who clearly had no lives. But there was another feeling rising within Autumn that gave her a strange sort of comfort. The feeling that no matter what, for reasons she had no comprehension of, she knew that she would get out of this situation. Taeyang squeezed her hand as they entered further into the room watching their step as they did.

"Now, according to my source, the box is somewhere in here." Taeyang instructed her, taking in the layout.

In the room itself there was a quaint oak dresser, an old vanity covered by an assortment of pictures, notes, snapshots, as well as an unmade bed. He let go of her hand and faced her as he grabbed her shoulders firmly.

"Autumn, I want you to check the vanity. I will check the closet, okay," he said pushing a loose strand of brown hair from her face.

"Okay, I'll do that," she answered before checking each drawer of the vanity cautiously.

Taeyang kept checking between what he was doing and what Autumn was touching. This room gave him a foreboding feeling, he prayed that the manuscript would show up quickly so that they could leave.

Taeyang sifted through the cluttered closet, there was a ton of Dark Star Seven merch. At the bottom of the closet in the left-hand corner was an unsealed brown cardboard box. He pulled it closer to get a better look, finding a handful of his personal effects, including a pair of his used boxers. He tossed it down in disgust.

"Those little-" he was cut off by a bang.

Autumn blanched as she dropped the drawer; on the floor there were razor blades, matches, used tampons, and a roll of duct tape that had tumbled out. Taeyang gripped her hand.

"I'll take care of this, leafy, just keep searching," he spoke before loosening his grip on her.

"Thanks. Just be careful, okay," she responded.

"I will. Don't worry," he replied as he refilled the drawer using a sock to cover his hand.

Taeyang finished filling the drawer and put it back in its place.

"Um, so where else could the manuscript be?" she asked before scanning the room.

Taeyang looked up at Autumn pondering over her question for a moment.

"I'll check under the bed," he stated trying to figure out where the manuscript could be.

Autumn checked under the vanity. Her mounds were visible and Taeyang tried not to look as he turned his attention to under the bed.

He searched until he found a box at the farthest corner, the image of Autumn's chest pestering his thoughts to the point where he left his place under the bed. She needed to get out of his sight right now.

"Autumn, can you go back downstairs and check there? Wait for me, once you are done," Taeyang instructed, not looking at her.

Autumn gave him a quizzical look as she stood up. However, she did as he asked her. Leaving the door ajar for Taeyang. He waited until he heard the last creaky step on the stairs before pulling out a box from under the bed. Taeyang unpacked the box. The manuscript was there, he checked each side including the binding before letting out a breath. The sasaengs hadn't done any damage. However, with the manuscript now secure it meant that Autumn would be leaving sooner. He sighed, he looked to the door that was ajar with only a fragment of light peeking through. A chill blazed across the room, he shivered at that or maybe the fear of being caught within the grip of deception was unbalancing his disposition. He couldn't hide it from her since he had no pockets big enough to stuff it away in, so he placed it out of sight beside the leg of the bedframe before leaving the room. He didn't want her to leave until he had read more of it.

Taeyang jogged back to Autumn who was paced outside fumbling with her hands. He grinned at her.

"It wasn't there, I'll check one more time. Can you do me a solid? I think that's the word people from your country use and get us both a coffee, Autumn?" Taeyang asked giving her a pan am smile.

"First of all, it's Canada not California. Second of all, are you feeling, okay? You've been acting weird," Autumn asked him.

"Pfft, are you stupid? Of course, I'm fine, I'm great actually. Just get the coffee, Autumn," he instructed before walking off.

"Jerk," she murmured watching his back as he left.

They sipped their drinks in silence for a few minutes. Autumn tapped her fingers against the table causing metallic thuds to drum out. The whooshing of the coffee machines and plates clattered in the background as she observed Taeyang. He remained silent staring at his untouched caramel brown napkin.

"I've been given another few days. But that's it. My agent made it clear that I'm on thin ice and I really don't feel like testing her on that one," she told him, stroking the rim of her coffee cup thoughtfully.

Taeyang stirred his coffee, nodding.

"Earth to Taeyang, are you listening?" she asked, waving her hand in his face.

Taeyang swatted her hand away before grabbing it.

"I heard you, Autumn. Don't put your hand in my face," he said to her before pushing her hand away.

"What's your problem? You've been nothing but a grouch since we left," Autumn asked, massaging her hand.

"I'm fine just trying to figure out what to do about your manuscript," he warned her before getting up to leave.

"Taeyang..." Autumn said as she watched him go outside.

He was blocking her out. This caused her to sigh sadly as she drank another sip of coffee before paying the bill and following him.

This whole thing was a mess. His feelings were muddled, Taeyang was glad that Autumn had additional time but then there's the sadness that would follow when she left for Canada which was strange considering that he didn't know her that well. Autumn observed him as they walked. Taeyang had been acting strange ever since they had left the sasaengs' house. Autumn couldn't put her finger on it, his face seemed troubled. Taeyang didn't tease her or bait her. He was silent, closed off, and barely ate or drank. She wanted to pry but she felt that it was best if he came to her in his own time. If she pushed him, she was afraid that he would never open up to her again.

Taeyang rubbed his temples, a headache swished inside of his mind, the feelings he was having only complicated their situation. Now that they were back at Heechul's place he had time to think but it only made him more emotional. He stepped into the empty living room noticing a piece of paper under a magenta coaster on the table.

Heechul had left the small note. He would be out with friends tonight cruising the Han River. Taeyang scrunched up the paper before dropping it into the waste bin. Autumn had attempted to spark up a conversation several times as they were coming back, but he couldn't talk to her right now. She didn't deserve his wrath. Taeyang kicked the table, quickly regretting it, as a series of shooting sharp pains started to attack his foot and ankle. There wasn't anything for him to do so he went upstairs to check on Autumn who was sleeping before leaving to pick up her manuscript that he had left in the rose bushes of the sasaengs' house earlier before going to meet with Autumn.

Chen stumbled out of the karaoke bar. In his drunken state he had called Taeyang who had just finished dropping off Autumn's manuscript at his friend's house. By the time Taeyang arrived, his manager was completely wasted. Chen's tie loosely hung around his white shirt collar. Taeyang rolled his eyes at the middle-aged buffoon as he attempted to flirt with another woman who was as drunk as he was and a lot younger. Taeyang watched the spectacle a little longer before marching up, and pulling his manager off her as he touched

72

the woman's firm keister. He tried to push Taeyang away, but he was easily overpowered. On the bright side, his manager would be so hungover he wouldn't even remember it. Taeyang lifted him up, the man was portly on top of being sweaty which didn't help. The smell of green onions mixed with alcohol made Taeyang wince. His personal hygiene was questionable at best. Taeyang put Chen's arm around his shoulders helping him down the road. Chen mumbled incoherently hanging on to Taeyang.

Part of him was tempted to leave Chen somewhere like a ditch. After what happened to Autumn, he didn't get the opportunity to confront Chen on it since there were almost always other people around. But now he was alone. He could find out more.

Taeyang along with Chen sat at the docks watching the ships sail to, and from the harbour. The salty air reminded Taeyang of his hometown. As a kid, he would accompany his uncle on fishing trips. Those were the best times from his childhood. Then life dropped the other shoe, he was such a selfish kid at the end. Taeyang exhaled, the past marked his heart, one he wished he didn't have at times. His thoughts returned to the present. Chen groaned, to the amusement of Taeyang.

"So why did you pretend to hire those guys on my behalf? How do you know about Autumn?" Taeyang asked.

Chen grumbled, "It was all money, she's juuuust the route." he slurred before burping.

Taeyang bit his lip repressing the urge to smack his manager. He knew about the money just not what it had been actually for. But he still couldn't figure out why Chen hadn't busted them over Autumn or what he had against her.

A horn sounded. The docks were breathtaking at night with the different lights, and exotic cargo coming in from all over the world. Taeyang looked to the man beside him. Chen never talked about his past. Even drunk, Taeyang couldn't get a proper answer out of the man. If he were honest, he wanted to hurt Chen for what he had done to Autumn but then they all would be busted. He sighed, looking at the horizon.

Autumn walked into a small town; the house felt claustrophobic. So, she decided to take a stroll. Past the thicket, trees, and flowers she found herself daydreaming. Her hand ached but it wasn't bleeding, she applied ointment to it this morning when she changed her bandage. She pressed her fingers against the cotton wrap, the sweat from her hand made the material greasy. "I'll clean it later," she thought to herself before narrowly missing a dirty puddle.

Autumn discovered a small market where vendors, and customers were bustling about. The place was amazing with the red, white thick signs with enclosed streets, and a chorus of powerlines hanging amongst the tops of the buildings. There were food stalls lining the streets – curry fish balls, Korean beef sandwich stands were a common sight here. Street food was cheaper than the restaurants a lot of the time and had a wider variety. Incense wafted through the streets as the sounds of bells, and rattling food carts harmonised around her.

Autumn liked the look of the kimchi. Fried foods weren't to her palate, and certain dishes were overly spicy. She watched the locals exchanging words. Most of the people who owned these stalls were elderly, but the vibe of this place was a mixture of traditional and modern. Autumn could see the allure of small places like this, there was a sereneness about them. She approached a stall that was selling what appeared to be coffee, with some rice, and pickled vegetables. There was a section offering what appeared to be dead bugs for free.

Seeing the deceased crickets made her feel a little bit nauseous but she didn't want to be rude, so she took one, eating it slowly as it crunched against her teeth. The elderly woman smiled, her teeth were worn down, and decayed but her attitude was very kind. Autumn smiled, swallowing hard; she heaved, feeling the cricket scraping against her throat as it went down.

She practically inhaled her iced coffee that she bought from the woman trying not to choke in the process. Dribbles of coffee ran down the corner of her lips onto her chin. She wiped her mouth using the back of her wrist. The woman handed her a handkerchief to use. She cleaned off her face before folding up the emerald material and handing it back to the woman. Autumn bowed before leaving.

Autumn bumped into a young woman whose hands were overloaded with bulging paper bags. She helped pick up a couple of bags that had tumbled to the ground before the woman slapped her hands back with a red fan as she glared at Autumn. This caused her to flinch and hold her wrapped hand. The woman gathered her stuff and then rushed off, causing Autumn to scratch her head. "That was weird," she thought watching the woman scurry through the crowd.

Autumn continued making her way around the market. Her nerves stimulated after bumping into that woman, she couldn't help but notice the different shadows, the little noises, the shifty eyes of the people going back and forth on the old and hole tracked road. Her guard was up, this created tension within her body making her purpose for being here a little more difficult than she intended it to be.

Bartering was also a common practice here as it turned out. In Canada, bartering in a store would be considered shameful but here a bargain was considered a battle of wills that only the most hardened professional could win. Autumn could feel another novel idea burrowing into her mind as she continued observing an exchange between two particularly fiery locals. She wondered what Taeyang was doing currently. He had not sent her a text or given her a call. Autumn started to miss his presence; he was like a prominent thorn in her side yet one that she found comforting after a while. Her blanket of peace was instantly snatched from under her as a sudden crash caused her turn, and when she did what she saw caused her face to turn ghostly pale.

Taeyang placed Chen on the bed almost tripping over stale beer cans. A dribble of brown liquid puddled on the floor. He sidestepped it before stretching his back. Chen was deadweight which didn't help Taeyang's ankle that protested at the abuse. Taeyang looked around, Chen's apartment was disgusting, old takeout piled up against the small TV set, soiled clothes were in an unorganised heap in the corner. The chairs he owned were covered with burn holes. Presumably from cigarette ends. Taeyang sighed, rubbing his neck. "Old bastard," he thought to himself as he looked at Chen who was sleeping like an itty-bitty baby on the futon.

Hyeon stood patiently outside of Heechul's house before knocking on the door.

"Hello there," he greeted before opening the door which was unlocked.

Hyeon removed his basil coloured flip flops before he stepped inside. The first clue that prodded his suspicion was when no one greeted him. Normally, Heechul would be chilling out in the living room if he didn't have work, or if an emergency came up. Hyeon took the liberty of getting to know Taeayang's friends. He was the closest to Taeyang out of the group.

Hyeon checked upstairs, but none of the rooms had any occupants.

"Autumn, Taeyang, it's Hyeon," he called out but received no response.

That was strange considering that Heechul was a bit of a homebody when his friends weren't in town. The rooms were empty, and the beds were cold. Taeyang hadn't left a note, and it seemed that Autumn had gone off somewhere.

Hyeon explored the kitchen.

A pink sticking to the fridge door caught his attention:

"Dear Taeyang /Heechul,

I've gone for a walk. I'll see you later.

Autumn."

Hyeon pulled the note from the fridge reading it over once more. His eyes became wide as he did so. Autumn was still injured from the last incident; she shouldn't be leaving the house without anyone until they get the sasaeng issue under control. Pulling on his hair, Hyeon sighed, thinking. This area didn't have much in regard to amenities but there was a small town nearby. If she went anywhere, it had to be there. Deciding to test his theory, he left the house and headed for the town.

By the time Hyeon found her she was sitting on a chair sipping some tea as her hands shook. Her face beyond pale and clammy as an older woman stood nearby. She seemed harassed; he didn't like it. He removed his sunglasses tucking them into his pocket, he scanned her over to make sure she had no damage to her body. She didn't notice him approaching her as she appeared to be lost in her own little world.

"Hey, Autumn. Are you okay?" he asked her.

Her trance was snatched from her a she looked at the young man.

She gave him a subdued smile as she answered,

"I don't know. I saw something that-t..." her eyes downcast as tears welled up.

Her summery glow wasn't present as she fondled the material of her dress. Her skin seemed withdrawn, as her huge blue orbs danced with tears teetering on them

"What happened?" he asked her to which she said,

"I-I can't.... It's too a-awful," she stammered.

"Okay, we don't have to talk about it if you don't want to. But I think it's time for us to go," he said as he kneeled down to look at her face to face.

Autumn nodded, and he stood up taking her hand into his own.

Her mind was numb. Hyeon felt pity for her, it was pretty obvious that whatever happened to her along with recent events was starting to weigh on her shoulders. Hyeon thought about what he could do to cheer her up then an idea tumbled into his brain. Quickly he changed direction and led her down towards a park. Autumn gave him a puzzled glance as they continued to travel onto a small dirt lane with trees hanging above them. The weather was topsy turvy today. She didn't have the correct clothing on but with the lack of predictable weather she wasn't certain if there was a correct way to dress for this place.

After they all got back to the house, none of them had really said much aside from Autumn and Taeyang since they were all tired. It was now time for dinner, so they decided to order out. Autumn was still processing the events of the day. But going to the park with Hyeon helped quite a bit. He bought her black sesame ice cream and they talked for a while. She felt gratitude for that as she sat back. Taeyang on the other hand chilled out watching a variety show. His body was sore from carrying around Chen. Both of them were sitting on the couch.

Hyeon came over handing them both their takeout orders and a bottle of water each.

"Thanks, Hyeon," Autumn said softly, her throat was considerably dry at this point.

The humidity at night was claustrophobic, sweat beaded on her chest as she sat there trying to ignore her discomfort. She just wanted to eat and then call it a night.

Autumn opened up the metallic takeout box. Steam poured out of it. Looking at her dinner she made a face before poking Taeyang's shoulder.

"I have three dates and chestnuts in my rice, but I never ordered anything relating to dates or chestnuts, Taeyang," she informed him giving the dates and chestnuts a prod with her finger.

Taeyang looked at them causing his eyes to double in size. He snatched the dates and chestnuts before tossing them across the room.

"Taeyang, what the hell was that for?" she asked glaring at him for poking his fingers in her dinner.

Hyeon giggled. "He's getting flustered because in our culture, dates and chestnuts symbolise female fertility. At the end of wedding ceremonies, the parents of the groom throw dates and chestnuts at the couple. The number of dates and chestnuts they catch will entail how many babies they will have," he elucidated, before giggling harder.

Now it was her turn to blush especially when she remembered something that Taeyang had encountered earlier.

Autumn had found Taeyang sitting by the window looking pensive. A book left half open, unloved and forgotten. She was in better spirits and ready to sort this out.

"So, about earlier…" she started to say when he shushed her.

"I don't want to talk about it. I'm fine like I said before, leafy," Taeyang said before getting up.

Autumn stood there looking at him as he went outside to get some air.

Taeyang went outside and stood under a tree. As soon as his back touched the bark, he felt three small balls hit him on the head. He picked them up from the ground and gasped. In his hand were three chestnuts. This creeped him out since he knew the meaning of their symbolism. Autumn's lack of knowledge on these customs didn't help either as she laughed at him through the window. He shook his head before throwing the chestnuts onto the ground.

After dinner Hyeon went to bed. But Autumn chose to stay up with Taeyang since she had slept earlier and didn't feel tired. The fan was blowing in the room. At this point, Autumn was wearing a pair of tight blue shorts and a white cami top with her hair in a top bun. She looked over at Taeyang who was watching TV.

His body looked delectable in his short black top and grey sweats. There was something animalistic about the way he sat there with his legs apart and chest heaving. Perspiration beading down his muscles like diamonds tumbling down the neck of an affluent dame being ravaged in a sensual manner. Autumn licked her lips. This heat was stirring something primal inside of her.

"Get a grip, Autumn! His ego is big enough as it is," she chided internally upon catching herself staring at him.

Meanwhile, Taeyang was having mixed emotions of his own as Autumn sat there in a tight top and shorts. Her curves were extenuated by the garments and her pliable parts seemed more touchable than usual. "Just a few inches over," he thought to himself. He hated feeling this way, like he had no control. She was a pristine angel, and yet also a stranger that could ruin his reputation. It didn't help that she had been staring at him as if he were covered in chocolate sprinkled with a touch of gold. He wasn't superstitious per se but after seeing those dates and chestnuts he didn't really want to risk taking this further. He opted to supplant his place on the couch as he went into the kitchen. Autumn sighed in relief feeling grateful that he had moved. To be quite honest she didn't know if she would be able to control herself around him. He looked too tempting. But hooking up with him would complicate things for her in a way that she couldn't handle.

They were both still hungry so they had ordered more food that had arrived a little while ago. Autumn opted for a simple dish; sushi. Taeyang entered the room with both of their meals. He handed Autumn hers before taking his own over to the window.

She thanked him before she unboxed her eel and salmon sushi, her mouth watered as she admired the perfect rice balls. She was just about stab a fork into them when a choking noise broke the silence. She whipped her head over to Taeyang. The area around HIS mouth was red and swollen, he started struggling to breathe. Autumn's eyes went wide as she dived over to his spot at the window and snatched the container from his hands. In bold letters at the back, "MAY CONTAIN TRACES OF SOY, MILK, AND PEANUT" which caused any remaining colour from her face to drain. "WHY DIDN'T HE READ THIS FIRST?!" she screamed in her head as she looked at him with absolute terror in her blue eyes. She didn't know that he was allergic to anything. His breathing was quickly becoming worse which triggered Autumn who flung the package and ran off to the kitchen to find an EpiPen.

From the living room Taeyang could hear her panicked destruction as she did her best to find the medicine he needed. Under normal circumstances, he would taunt her for acting like an unhinged bull but right now he was trying his best not to choke to death. Autumn knocked over tea towels, and everything else in her wake. He started gasping for air as he moved from the window to the kitchen. His face become more inflamed, which added to her growing terror as she caught sight of him. His eyes were watery, red, and swelling up fast. Taeyang's breaths coming out in congested mucus-laden wheezes as he begged her with his eyes to help him. This caused something in her to snap as she went into a full desperate rampage.

Destroying every single cupboard until she found an EpiPen. Practically she ripped off the cap from the pen, broke the seal, and stabbed it into his leg. Her hands shaking, her mind completely descending into a void of the worst possible scenarios. He collapsed onto the floor with the pen still in his leg.

"TAEYANG!" she screamed as she caught him.

Autumn panicked as she watched his body twitch and the swelling continue.

"Taeyang, please stay awake!" she begged him as she saw his eyes closing.

"Hyeon!" she screamed from the top of her lungs.

She held onto Taeyang's hand. Squeezing it as she cried. He was barely conscious at this point.

"Where the heck is he?!" she fretted gripping his hand harder. He moaned at that causing her to give him some room as she loosened her grip on his hand.

Autumn's heart ached seeing him like this. She felt so powerless. Taeyang had been able to protect her on so many occasions and now here he was in trouble and there was nothing that she could do.

"I am s-so...s-sorry...." she whispered as she bawled her eyes out.

Taeyang couldn't think. He struggled to breathe. The image of his mother came before him suddenly. He wanted to cry. He missed her terribly, sometimes he wondered if he was remembering the right woman. He didn't have any pictures of her. His father torched them in a rage after he found out what she had done. A small fragment of him resented his father for that. These feelings had a habit of coming and going.

His mother's voice came to him, she was a source of strength. Despite her shortcomings he loved her.

"Fight it, Taeyang," she whispered before vanishing.

"M-mother," he muttered trying to breakthrough his delirium. Autumn stroked his head gently as she screamed for Hyeon for what felt like the millionth time.

The image of Autumn's distorted figure started coming to him next. She looked glorious with thick longish brown strands, her blue eyes sparkled, she seemed a bit older. He did his best to reach out to her but his limbs were so heavy with pins and needles stabbing each nerve as he moved. She wasn't speaking but she had three children around her who were smiling and laughing as they all played. The smell of magnolias filled his nose. Before he knew what he was doing, he started running faster and faster trying to reach her, she seemed to fade farther with every footstep, along with the children, as pain filled his soul.

"Please don't leave, stay with me, leafy, I can't lose anyone else. Please leafy!" he pleaded.

She just giggled as she dissolved into the light with the three children. His hand caught the light before everything became dark and cold.

Hyeon ran into the kitchen. His face was flushed, and he looked damp.

"Autumn, what are you yelling for-" his words dropped from his mouth as he saw Taeyang on the ground and her reddish tearstained face peered up at him.

"H-he had a... a reaction. I-I gave him an EpiPen but he's still not out of it!" she explained through sobs.

Heechul came rushing in just getting back from his Han River shenanigans.

"What happened?" he asked in Korean.

"Allergic reaction," Hyeon replied, still dazed.

Autumn curled her own hand around Taeyang's tighter, focusing solely on him. Heechul grabbed her arm pulling her away from Taeyang as Hyeon snapped out of his shock.

"We need to go to the hospital. This won't help him; we need to go now!" Heechul snapped in English as he pulled up Autumn who was hysterical.

Hyeon picked Taeyang up and carried him to the car whilst Heechul rushed behind them with a distraught Autumn.

They waited in the emergency room, Hyeon sat on a hard metallic leather chair trying not to check his phone whilst Heechul kept glancing at the large clock. Hyeon had informed the others of what had occurred a little while ago. There was still no sign of a doctor, and the sight of Taeyang looking dead disturbed them both. Autumn had barely spoken since the car ride, but she wasn't crying now.

Her tight clothes dripped from the downpour they had been caught in as they desperately rushed their friend into the ER of Bumin Hospital. They parked farther away because there was only one parking spot left. Taeyang was taken from them as soon as they hit the reception and whisked off to another department. This left them where they currently stopped, in the waiting room, drenched, upset and impatient.

Hyeon looked towards Autumn who appeared to be on the verge of a stroke. She was pacing back and forth creating a dark scuff on the floor. Her shaky hand against her mouth as she tried her best not to freak out. But internally she was a total wreck.

"It's just an allergic reaction. This happens every day. He'll be okay, at least I hope," she whispered to herself forgetting Hyeon and Heechul's presence entirely.

Seeing Taeyang in such a bad state scared her in a way that she had never felt before. Autumn never wanted to be in that position again.

Hyeon was growing agitated by this point. A blend of worry, weariness, shock, and the urge to yell at these damn doctors for taking this amount of time collided in his mind. "Autumn! Quit pacing, he'll be fine, we're all worried but this won't help anyone!" he snapped.

This provoked Autumn who stopped pacing and glared at the younger man.

"How do you know?! Are you a doctor?! Just because he's an idol doesn't mean that he's invincible! You saw him Hyeon, he looked dead!" she hoarsely shouted with tears brimming in her eyes.

Heechul looked between the two of them,

Images of Taeyang's lifeless body burrowed behind her blue eyes, seeing him like that had shifted a piece of her heart pushing her greatest fear to the forefront. Her breathing became heavier as a vice grip formed around her throat and chest. She fell to her knees struggling to breathe as her body shook. Hyeon and Heechul rushed over to her.

"Autumn!" both exclaimed in unison.

Autumn gripped her chest. She clenched her eyes shut, thinking of Taeyang's smile. The joy that gave her was immense. In her mind, he was okay, he was there beside her.

Neither Heechul or Hyeon knew what to do but Hyeon tried to comfort Autumn.

"Autumn, he'll be fine, I promise. You trust him, right? If he means as much to you as you say, then you should believe in him enough to know that he wouldn't let something as minor as an allergy take him out," Hyeon said, rubbing her back carefully.

After a few minutes Autumn calmed down enough to stand back up.

"T-thank you," she whispered to them both.

A young nurse approached the trio, a notably small woman who had her black hair in a slick ponytail and perfectly manicured French nails. She had clean green scrubs on and was wearing framed glasses.

"How is he?" Hyeon asked his voice gravelly.

Autumn gave the nurse a pleading look as Heechul held her arm.

The nurse scrunched her dark brows together, her expression changing from hurried and energetic to serious contemplation.

"He had a serious reaction, we've given him a steroid and liquid through an IV, he's been on oxygen which he has responded well to. He's awake and rather sarcastically answering our questions now. So, if you want to see him you can go ahead," she relayed giving Autumn a concerned glance.

"Is your friend there, okay?" the nurse asked in Korean.

Hyeon looked at Autumn who appeared sickly pale, and her eyes were puffy and bloodshot.

"Yes, she is just upset," Hyeon assured the nurse.

Autumn almost fainted upon hearing the news that Hyeon had translated for her. She had been on the edge of terror and adrenaline for the last four hours and didn't know how much more her body was willing to endure. They followed the nurse down the hallway passing various rooms, and a few patients who were hanging around. Autumn rushed past the nurse when she heard his laugh. That full, baritone laugh with just a touch of silliness that she had grown to know and care about.

Taeyang was sitting up in bed, the redness around his mouth had faded and he seemed more alert than before but with sluggishness still lingering. He had an IV drip attached to his arm. A nurse was talking to him, before handing him a piece of paper which he signed before handing it back. Autumn was relieved but also in awe, he looked incredibly sweet, and innocent as he sat there, his wall was down, and his blue hair was in a mess. Taeyang looked at her lovingly, her smile intensified as she fought back tears. His black roots beginning to show on his head. "I hope he lets his natural hair grow out," she wished internally as she stared at him.

Autumn couldn't help herself as she fully entered the room. She was just so relieved to the point where she tackled him as she did her best not to cry all over his chest. Her perception of Taeyang had shifted upon seeing his sweet side resurfacing. She'd never let him go and was beyond thrilled that he was okay and not near the edge of death anymore. She felt eyes staring at them and moved away quickly. Embarrassment replaced her loving relief as she backed off. He smirked, enjoying her embarrassment.

"Really, leafy? I mean I know you can't get enough of my godlike body but there are people here," he playfully scolded.

A look of horror came across her face at that as she was about to deny the allegation when Soon Woo strolled in with a fresh hickey and coffee. Hyeon shook his head as Heechul just laughed, whilst Autumn waved happily at him, relieved that the attention was off her. He winked at her; she rolled her eyes in response but the cheeky grin that was now on her face never left.

That lusty fool was a sight for sore eyes. He looked pleased with himself, and she decided that when she had the chance she would like to write about his sexual adventures.

"Who am I kidding eh? That wouldn't be a novel, that would be an epic," she mused as she was handed a cup of fresh coffee.

It seemed to be a different concoction than she'd had before. The smell was richer, and the cream had a fluffiness to it.

"Um Soon? What kind of coffee is this?" she asked him with suspicion lacing her tone.

"Its dalgona coffee. Try it, it's very popular here," he said and that was enough for her, so she took a tiny sip.

Her eyes lit up as soon as the liquid hit her tongue, it was absolutely delicious, and she found herself downing it like a possessed racoon.

Taeyang poked fun at Soon Woo, "So, I take it that another conquest was made? I guess I'm not the only one with an injury,"

Soon Woo tapped his nose with his finger before answering, "Maybe, but that's between me and my partner, I don't lick and tell, you know,"

He gave Taeyang a knowing wink.

They all sweat dropped at that with Autumn turning multiple shades of red as she felt grossed out by his wicked and unfettered tongue.

The way he licked the ridge of the cup before taking a big sip told her that he was goading them and enjoying every second of it. She stuck her tongue out at him before turning her attention back to Taeyang who looked tired. She handed him a cup of coffee.

"This should help," she told him.

He swallowed the brown liquid, belching shortly after to her disgust.

"That's good coffee," he commented letting the liquid mix within his throat.

"Yeah, it is," Autumn replied, placing her cup down on the floor.

It really was tasty coffee. Speaking of which...

"What you did was generous, thank you Soon Woo," Autumn said before getting up to bow.

Soon blushed at the gesture before bowing in return. They all started laughing. A nurse came in, shooing them away from the bed, as she checked Taeyang over.

"I figured that you guys would need it after what Hyeon told us. I may be a lusty fool, but I do care about the people I deal with. Once we are done here, we should head out. The weather is getting unsightly," he said before going over to the window to open the curtains.

Rain was pelting against the jaded glass; fat drops of rain streaked down it. Autumn frowned as she watched the downpour. She had no desire to go back out into that.

Chapter Five

A Letter From Afar

Taeyang was still feeling shaky but managed to pat Autumn's head in easy motions as she sat beside him on the white cotton covers of the hospital bed. He had a lot to think about, hearing his mother stirred something odd in him. Mainly the hole that she had left. Then seeing an older version of Autumn stirred something new in him. A feeling of belonging. Taeyang wanted to go home but the hospital wanted him to stay a little longer to be on the safe side. His bandmates had visited before deciding to give Taeyang and Autumn some alone time. Heechul had work so he had to go. His face was still sore but no longer red or swollen. He brushed it aside. At least he was alive. That's all that really mattered.

Autumn stroked his chest. She was completely wiped out emotionally. All she wanted to do was bask in his peaceful presence.

"So, how do you feel?" she asked him breaking the silence.

He yawned, "I'm tired but I'll live, leafy," he told her before placing his hand gently on her back.

Her skin felt cold which bothered him. Her blue eyes had purple shadows under them and her skin seemed duller. It was clear that last night had taken its toll on her. He felt guilt forming inside of his chest. Taeyang should have checked his order last night but he was focusing so much on trying not to pounce on Autumn's body that he didn't even think about it. Seeing how distraught she was made him feel fiercely protective which only added to the turbulence of his thoughts.

"I have things I need to think about more, but I am glad that I didn't die," he admitted out loud.

Autumn moved closer to him, the way his voice lowered when he said that made her want to engulf him in a hug. He was such an enigma at times, but during moments like this when he wasn't evading questions and was being straightforward it was comforting in a wholesome sense.

"For what it's worth, I'm glad that you are still here. I thought you had died, for a minute. When you started talking about your mother and begging for her," she said softly.

He looked down at his lap, the tips of his ears turning red.

She bit her lip before continuing, "Don't get me wrong, anyone else would have done the same thing. I've had times where my nightmares have caused me to yell out for my father."

He rubbed circles on Autumn's back in response.

They remained silent for a few minutes before Autumn thought of something.

"So, how was it being a ghost? Do you see anything interesting?" she inquired, a portal of questions filling the vastness of her mind's landscape.

"I'm not religious. The idea of ghosts is crazy in my opinion but my mother was definitely there. There's no other way in which I can explain it, leafy. She was talking to me when I... well, you know," when he spoke his voice cracked.

"If that's what you feel, then it is what it is. Don't rush for answers, they will find you eventually. You've got friends who love you, and fans, at least the non-crazy ones, who love you to death. It's not all bad, and I bet she's so proud of you," Autumn said sincerely.

His eyes took on a tender glow as he looked into her own. One she found herself flying into, the pull felt entrenched in her soul – it frightened and invigorated her entire being. Taeyang pierced her soul with his gaze, part of him was tempted to kiss her but he shook it off since someone could walk in at any moment. Plus, his bladder was giving him other ideas.

"I need the bathroom. I'll be back," he said, gently pushing her off him.

As Taeyang walked off she smacked his ass playfully before laughing hysterically. A tender blush came over his face as he glared at her before going off to pee.

"So, how did it feel to see her again?" Autumn asked Taeyang once he had returned.

Taeyang's experience reminded her of her own father. As a little kid she wished to see him, the more summers passed the less she had that feeling. He was at peace, what right did she have to disturb his rest? If there was a world following this one, then she knew in heart of hearts that they would be reunited.

Autumn's name being called caused her to look into Taeyang's beautiful hazel orbs that burned into her skull.

"Autumn? Autumn? Are you okay?" Taeyang asked her, his eyes filled with concern.

"Sorry, yeah, I was just thinking of my own dad," Autumn said trying to hide her sadness.

"Oh, that makes sense," he responded.

"Maybe if my mother had been alive, I wouldn't be as stubborn," he said trying to lighten his mood.

"Can I get that in writing?" Autumn asked as her smile emerged.

"Ha ha, very cute Autumn," Taeyang quipped back, as he flicked her hair.

Autumn pushed his chest before she responded, "Honestly. Mr Arrogant, I don't think you would be the same if you weren't a hard head." she pinched his ear playfully.

He held his ear pretending to be hurt by her actions. She mouthed something along the lines of 'get over it'.

"You are one to talk, miss I know everything," he teased, poking her shoulder.

She stuck her tongue out at him which he pulled on with his forefinger and thumb. Autumn made a disgusted face; the skin of his fingers was salty. She pulled his fingers away giving him a dirty look.

This made him smirk as he rubbed his saliva-stained fingers on his chest.

"So, how's your face feeling, eh? Is it still sore?" she verbally prodded once she composed herself.

He shook his head. "It's better, and at least it's not permanent. Plus, I got the chance to be waited on for a change," he remarked.

She snorted at that; his sense of entitlement was annoying but also funny.

"How is that different from any other day, eh?" Autumn teased.

"Tch. I do everything for myself," Taeyang replied.

"Really? you haven't made a meal for yourself once since I've met you, I bet you don't even know how to use a pan," she jabbed playfully with mocking indignance.

He scoffed at her. "I can cook, I just choose not to since I can get underlings to do it for me,"

"Yeah, likely story, Taeyang," Autumn poked his chest.

He grinned even more, the muscles beneath his eyes stretching further back.

"Are you challenging me, leafy? Because I can tell you right now who would lose. Unlike, most people I could mention, here we take food seriously. I can make kimchi, bibimbap, seaweed soup, grilled fish, and basically any Korean recipe you throw at me," he bragged.

"Alright then, how about later today? We can even get Soon Woo and a couple of the guys involved if you want," she proposed hoping that he would rise to the challenge.

"Okay, you're on, leafy!" he answered before flicking her nose.

Autumn glared at him as she rubbed the now sore spot.

Taeyang and Autumn snuck into his dorm with the help of Hyeon and Taemin.

There was something that Taeyang wanted to show her.

"I intended on showing you this before but it slipped my mind. Our group gets fan mail, the people at our company sift through it before sending it to us," he told her as he searched through a small plastic black box.

Autumn looked at him curiously.

Taeyang handed her a letter that had silver ink scribbled across it from the box.

"Despite the rumours being disproven there are some of fans who have decided to ship us both. One of them sent you a letter. I don't know how they know your name but it seems legit.," Taeyang told her.

Autumn read the letter, trying to resist the urge to convulse with laughter. She had to give his fans credit, they had very furtive imaginations. The fan had included snaps of her and Taeyang. The pictures fans had snagged were less than flattering, her hair looked windswept and unwashed so she was surprised that anyone would write to her after seeing her like that. Taeyang noticed her eyes as they critiqued her picture. He never had her down as someone who was insecure or cared about her looks.

"Hey, don't worry about those pictures, you look fine. Also, I'm sure that you are used to receiving letters and other forms of mail by now," he spoke, thinking back to all of the times that he himself had been the subject to the lavishing attention of various admirers.

"Trust me, I am, most of them are about the books usually. Nothing pertaining to me, excluding the odd marriage request and a few affectionate notes which are usually quite sweet," she told him trying to hide her embarrassment.

Upon hearing this his muscles tensed up. He was well aware of the fact that she had fans and was successful, but didn't think that they would be attracted to her in the romantic sense. It was difficult to imagine another man praising her pictures, imagining her, and falling for her the way his fangirls did with him. His clenched his jaw trying to quell the sudden anger that was bubbling up.

"Why? Why do I feel an intense jealousy?" the question bubbled in his mind but was quickly shot down by his ego. "It's nothing. Just adrenaline," he thought to himself.

Taeyang then recalled something that had happened earlier. As they were walking, a fangirl had run up to them. He had been disguised but she still recognised him. Taeyang could have sworn that Autumn's face had taken on a dark aura, as if she was trying to pulverise the girl with her azure eyes. That provided an opening for another quandary. If hypothetically, she liked him, and he liked her in the same regard, how could they work without outsiders getting in-between them? Taeyang loved his sane fans, and despite not vocalising it much, he knew that she loved her fans with the same strength.

"Can I even have a relationship at this point?" he asked himself feeling the weight of this situation on his broad shoulders.

The sasaengs were a struggle, but what would happen if all of his saner fans found out? Would they accept her? Would he be placing her in more danger? She has already gone through so much because of him, would it be fair to put her through more? No matter how he looked at it the prospects were glum. Regardless, of who he chose to have as a girlfriend, they would never be able to have a normal and peaceful life together. Unless they left and he went to Canada with her. But then he would be away from everything that he knows. Would that be fair?

Taeyang's thoughts were interrupted by Autumn.

"Um Taeyang, in future, be careful what you eat. Also, I'm sorry that I freaked out, you needed help and if I hadn't wasted so much time panicking you might not have needed to go to the hospital. It's my fault and I promise that it won't happen again," she said with remorse evident in her voice.

He looked at her confused. This wasn't her fault. Not at all.

"Stop leafy, it's not your fault. It's no one's fault. What happened was an accident, nothing more, nothing less. Don't feel bad about it, I'm not upset about that like I have already moved on from it. It sucked, we all got a fright but I'm here and I'm fine so it worked out," he said giving her a weak smile.

She leaned her chin onto his shoulder, he blew on her solemn face. They giggled; his eyes sparkled as he stared into hers. He looked shockingly beautiful and innocent.

"So, about your mother, what was she like? I bet that she was pretty," Autumn mused, waiting for his reaction.

"My mother had black hair and blue eyes from what I can remember, but when I died, I heard her voice not so much saw her face," Taeyang said, shifting in his seat.

"Oh okay," Autumn said looking at him sadly.

Taeyang looked at her. He could tell that she was thinking about her own father. Neither of them had been blessed in that department. For some reason it hurt him more seeing that expression on her face. He had to make it stop so he leaned forward and hugged her hesitantly. This surprised Autumn who remained still at first before slowly wrapping her arms around him. He felt soft against her despite his muscular body. She melted into his embrace and he relaxed at that. So warm and welcoming. It felt like home. It was the kind of feeling she felt every time she was in Canada. Taeyang held her close, she felt nice in his arms. They enjoyed each other's vibe for a minute.

"Taeyang, what happened between your parents?" Autumn asked him as they pulled away from each other.

He sighed, wondering where to begin. "I don't want to go into too much detail but my mother had an affair. She committed suicide over the shame and then my father joined her," Taeyang relayed to Autumn, who looked horrified.

"Oh god Taeyang, I'm so sorry," she said as tears welled up in her eyes.

Taeyang wiped her tears away before they could fall, he hugged her again but without hesitation this time.

"It was a long time ago. Please don't cry over it. I think you've done enough crying lately. Honestly, leafy, you're pumping out more water than our dorm's bidet," he joked trying to lighten the mood.

Autumn laughed at that before gently smacking his back but neither of them broke the hug.

"Why are we doing this again?" Taeyang remarked as himself, Soon Woo, Hyeon, and Autumn were gathered in the kitchen of Hyeon's parents' house.

They were barely ever home and Heechul's kitchen was still being fixed after the damage that Autumn had inflicted.

"Because Mr Smartass, you agreed to this challenge, so here we are," she instructed before going to her station.

"We have stuff to do leafy, like getting your manuscript and our group has signings to practise for," he drawled as his nerves were starting to flare up.

"Smh, this will only take an hour, I promise, now let's get started," she said before setting the plastic timer onto the grey marble countertop.

The ingredients were laid out across each side of the kitchen counter. Since there was only one cooker, they would need to take turns using it.

"I can't believe I agreed to this clown show," he muttered, feeling completely ridiculous in his pink apron.

"We each have a dinner recipe that we need to make. Whoever makes the one that looks closest to its original picture, is the victor," she instructed them before clicking on the timer. They all scuffled around.

Autumn grabbed the plug for the blender, the shape of it was odd to her. She would never get used to these kinds of things when travelling. A larger hand came over her own grabbing the plug and adjusted it before putting it into the socket.

"Thanks," she said turning to face Taeyang who smirked at her, and gave her a cheeky look.

"What? It's a weird plug," she argued.

"I thought that you would know all about inserting things, Autumn," Taeyang leaned down and whispered.

This made her shiver before she glared,

"At least the things that I insert are big enough to fill the socket."

Taeyang licked his lips "I've seen bigger. I've been bigger," he lowered his voice even further as he said the last part.

Enjoying how bothered Autumn was getting by his insinuations.

"Shut up, pervert," Autumn said trying to calm her quivering soul.

"Think of me. When you handle those cucumbers. With those dainty little hands of yours," Taeyang taunted before moving away from her.

Autumn glared at him; his face smugly victorious as he looked at her.

"Jerk," she muttered under her breath as her heart raced.

He had won this battle. She wouldn't let him win the challenge.

Taeyang cut the cucumber, carrot, red onion, before using a vegetable grater to make strings. He placed them into a bowl arranging them into their own sections. Soon Woo kept snacking whilst Hyeon busied himself with his salmon dish. Autumn regained her focus and started working through the recipe. She did her best to block out the nonsensical chatter in the background. A pet peeve of hers was having people hovering whilst she cooked but since she had challenged Taeyang, she would tolerate it.

Taeyang lightly tapped her shoulder before handing her a tub of gochujang.

"We use this for flavour and spice," he mentioned before popping another carrot stick into his mouth.

Looking at him she honestly wondered where he was able to stuff it all. Autumn looked at the paste sceptically. She decided to skip the cookbook and use her own intuition. Putting the book to the side she cracked an egg and worked away. Taeyang caught a glimpse of her side, noticing that she had put the cookbook aside. He had to admit, she at least deserved a point for ambition.

Meanwhile Soon Woo was busy sampling the tofu soup that he had just finished heating up in the microwave. He didn't care about the challenge. He just wanted the food.

"It's orgasmic, the sweet and sour with a touch of spice makes my tongue very happy," he chirped.

Autumn rolled her eyes as she laughed. The man just had to interject sex into everything.

"Down boy, honestly Soon, not everything revolves around one bodily function you know. There are other things in life like art and travelling," she said as she added some spices to her mixture.

"But my dearest Autumn, without sex none of these things would exist. I have lust for a list of different things, but women are the main one, for they are my art, and I am their artist," he said before grabbing her hand and spinning her around.

Autumn shook her head laughing at how cheesy his English was before she pushed him away. The man was ridiculous.

Whilst everything was cooking and Hyeon was burning his fish, Autumn took this as an opportunity to talk to Taeyang. She was curious about Soon Woo.

"Hey Taeyang, have you ever met Soon Woo's girlfriends?" she whispered to Taeyang who 'tch'ed before answering.

"I wouldn't call them girlfriends. But no, I haven't. He's probably bedded half of Seoul at this point," he stated with a catty humour in his voice.

She gave him a "Jealous much?" look as he continued.

"We had a physical a couple of months ago and he ended up being the fittest one out of all of us," he informed her and she couldn't help but notice the twitch his eyebrow made at that.

"Tell me about it, he seems to have endless energy," she said finding his reaction entertaining.

"The wrong kind usually," Taeyang muttered.

Hyeon interjected by handing Taeyang a letter.

"I forgot to give you this. It came yesterday," he said in Korean.

"Idiot!" Taeyang responded smacking him on the head lightly with the letter.

Taeyang checked the address of the letter. It was sent from Jeju Island, his home. He ripped open the top before pulling out the letter. He unravelled it, and instantly he stiffened up. It was from his brother Jung-Hwa who wanted to see him to catch up and congratulate him on his latest single. Taeyang read the letter over four times before folding it back up. He held it gently within his hands, the grits of sand on the paper reminded him of the adventures he had around Jeju Island with his little brother when they were younger. Before they became distant.

Autumn observed Taeyang's reaction. Any thoughts of besting him left her mind. It was clear that he needed to deal with whatever situation the letter had brought up. His brown eyes had taken on a look of sadness but also surprise. It was evident that whoever wrote the letter meant a lot to him.

"Taeyang, forget this stupid challenge. Soon Woo cheated by using instant tofu soup, Hyeon has burnt his fish and I botched the recipe. Wherever we have to go, let's just do it!" she spoke up, before approaching him.

Taeyang turned his attention to her, overcome with surprise.

"Admitting defeat, are we?" he asked giving her a knowing look.

"Nope, but I know when to give up. Plus, this seems more important," Autumn responded giving him a small smile.

"It's my brother, he wants to see me," Taeyang informed her as he thumbed the letter.

"I see, well Heechul told me about your parents but not your brother," she explained.

"If you knew, why did you ask me about them before?" Taeyang questioned her.

"Because I wanted to hear it from you," she told him as she looked into his eyes.

"Autumn..." he said, smiling at her softly.

"Look, I know it's a lot for you to handle. But you won't have to do it by yourself," Autumn said before rubbing his arm gently.

"Right, well it will only take a couple of hours by plane," Taeyang stated, his voice neutral as he did.

She lowered her hand nearly stumbling as he clenched it.

Taeyang insisted on taking a private jet. It was faster, and hassle free with no risk of the media finding out. Autumn was still holding his hand as they sat side by side on the plane. Taeyang was burning holes into the back of the chair in front of them where Heechul was sitting – he had agreed to come along with them on this excursion. She squeezed his hand trying to comfort him. He didn't like planes. They were coffins with wings as far as he was concerned but this was the fastest way to Jeju. "Oh Taeyang, why don't you just drop the pride for a minute and talk to me," she thought watching his face flinch from time to time. He held her hand tighter. She could have sworn that when the jet bumped, she saw his skin lose all of its colour.

Chapter Six

Adventures On Jeju Island

They arrived on Jeju Island, Heechul left the jet first before Taeyang stumbled behind him. Grateful to be off that flying death trap. Autumn trailed behind them both flexing her aching hand. Taeyang had squeezed the life out of her now porcelain white fingers.

"What do you think, Autumn?" Heechul asked her stretching his arms into the air.

She smiled as the three of them walked through the large island.

"It's nice here," she replied. The weather was warm, the plants were vibrant, and the waters brushed against the white sands in gentle whooshing motions.

The scenery reminded her of Hawaii.

Heechul grinned, soaking up the rays as he walked. Taeyang kept quiet, glaring at Heechul intermittently.

"Autumn, Taeyang, I'm off now. There are a few things I have to do before we go. Meet me at the museum once you done here," Heechul told them before walking off.

"Alright, be safe Heechul," she told him as Taeyang gave a disinterested grunt.

Taeyang strolled along the concrete road walking parallel to the luscious white beach. Autumn followed a few feet behind him, she was lost in her own thoughts at this point. She would have to leave soon and still didn't have her manuscript. "I'm going to miss Taeyang, more than I thought I would," she thought repressing the sudden urge to cry.

Taeyang looked over his shoulder creasing his brow. He didn't understand why she was suddenly upset. But he didn't like it.

"Come on leafy, you're even slower than usual today," he baited her waiting for a response but received nothing in return.

She was lost in her own head.

He rolled his eyes before he stopped walking and turned to face her.

She felt Taeyang's muscular chest before she saw that he had stopped walking.

He looked down at her unamused.

"Look, Autumn. Whatever is going on with you, just spit it out already, I don't have all day," Taeyang spoke, his patience dwindling as quickly as the tide.

Autumn turned to the beach; the breeze swept through her dress. The golden rays of the sun reflected off of her tanned complexion giving her the visage of the Greek goddess, Athena.

She sighed and contemplated whether or not to tell him. "It's nothing. I just want to be alone for a while," she admitted, not looking at him.

This further aggravated him, and before he could stop himself, he rather juvenilely, yanked her hair which caused her to smack him on the shoulder.

Taeyang's patience snapped. He had expected her to say something not smack him.

"You know what, forget it!" he huffed at her before storming off.

Autumn stomped her left foot before shouting after him,

"What's your problem?!"

"The same as usual, you!" he yelled back.

"Fine! You're just an immature brat anyway! With a bad dye job!" she yelled again feeling satisfied with her remark.

Taeyang stopped at that, the air surrounding him became charged as the chorus of quacking goosanders around them fell silent. Autumn gulped stepping away as her cheeky smile vanished. His angry frown formed into a devilish leer; his eyes were narrow as ruby flames sparked within his pupils. He prowled back to Autumn's side as she increased her pace backwards. Fear prickling across her body with every crunch that her steps made.

"Insulting my personality is one thing, Autumn..." he said. His voice was remarkably calm which roused her suspicions, whilst terrifying her at the same time.

He stopped dead, just a breath away from her face as she froze up.

"But. Don't. Insult. My. Hair." he whispered, punctuating each word with a firm poke to her cheek.

She glared at his finger but felt relieved that he wasn't sincerely angry at her. Taeyang leaned into her ear causing her breath to hitch.

"Unless you want to be bald when you go back to Canada," he whispered devilishly.

Autumn gasped as her blue eyes widened, she grasped her hair before shaking her head vehemently.

Taeyang grinned as he flicked her hair before leaving.

Taeyang and Autumn re-joined Heechul at the Bunker de Lumiere's. Taeyang's brother's house was not that far from here. Autumn felt unadulterated amazement from the moment she stepped inside. If she wasn't won over by the fact that this museum was disguised as a mountain and trees on the outside. But the murals on the ceiling deeply touched her creative soul. Taeyang on the other hand, looked as if he was being held against his will with a gun to his head. He checked his phone. Dusty paintings weren't his thing at all. Still, he wasn't ready to face his brother yet.

Autumn on the other hand, was entranced by one exhibit in particular. It was a boxlike structure with white small flowers budding from a tree that contrasted with a light navy-blue background. She considered every edge and corner. A sinking feeling came over her suddenly, the scene reminded her of a moment from her manuscript where the elderly couple end up saying goodbye. She missed her manuscript dearly. The characters had become like friends in her darkest hours, but she had faith that Taeyang would find it. Taeyang decided to get some refreshments whilst Autumn was busy looking at the art, and Heechul was busy flirting with a couple of American women who were giggling and exchanging embarrassed glances.

Taeyang handed her some peanut ice cream, Autumn looked up at him, her lips curled up as she grinned from ear to ear. Such a simple gesture warmed her heart considerably.

"Thank you, Tae," she said before nibbling on her frosty treat.

Her eyes sparkled as the sweet taste hit her taste buds, and she eagerly took another bite.

"It's a speciality here. They use peanuts from Udo Island, it's a smaller island but it's right next this one," he told her before sipping on his coffee.

She grinned, offering him some of the ice cream.

"I'm allergic to peanuts, Autumn, remember?" he said pushing her offer away.

"Oh shoot, that's right, I'm so sorry," she said putting some distance between them.

If she were honest, she had done her best to block out the memory of his allergic reaction – it was too painful for her to re-experience.

Taeyang laughed, Autumn had ice cream layering her top lip as she finished her treat. He pushed her head up to look at him before he grabbed a napkin out of his pocket and cleaned her mouth. She shied away; he was looking at her in a manner that made her heart skip. His eyes held such a tender care in them that it made her feel naked. He retracted the napkin as he felt himself fall into her eyes. The blue of them pulled at his soul and he found them hard to resist. Taeyang looked away as he grabbed her now finished pot of ice cream and went to find a bin. But also to calm himself down.

Autumn approached an exhibit before looking up and gasping; her eyes wide with curiosity. Standing before them was a marvellous piece. The picture was a landscape of little houses on a hill with yellow grass and small bushes. The roofs were a variety of shades, but the red roof caught her eyes the most. In the picture there was a faceless man standing. The lines were squiggly but added to the rustic feel of the image it was portraying. She found herself revelling in its complexity.

Taeyang watched Autumn, his boredom dissolved the further into the museum they went. Between Heechul being shot down by women, and Autumn's childlike joy and constant blabbering over the different works of art Taeyang found himself smiling more. He felt a tug on his shirt, Autumn was pulling him to another exhibit. Taeyang laughed at that.

"Autumn you are starting to sound like Hyeon," he teased.

Autumn flicked her hair back before she strutted off, the grin never leaving her mouth. Then it occurred to her.

"Wait. Where is Heechul?" Autumn asked furrowing her brows.

Taeyang smirked, shrugging.

"He is around here somewhere, either flirting with some poor girl or pissing her off," he relayed before walking onward.

Autumn chortled at the image of Heechul trying to be a ladies' man. She then abandoned that thought as another exhibit caught her eye.

"Even the floors have art on them," Autumn shrilled, clasping her soft hands together.

Taeyang looked down at their feet. Beneath them were different shades of blue, and green, with circular oranges that spread out to flowers of white with dots of yellow in the middle. Taeyang traced each pattern with his foot. Each line was done with remarkable precision. Taeyang looked back at Autumn. Her happiness was very infectious, he found it difficult to be moody, and uncaring when she was prancing about like a happy deer playing in the long grasses of the Seoul Forest. Her love for art was absolutely precious. Just another thing about her that made him happy.

They were eventually re-joined by Heechul who came over with his tail between his legs after another group of women shot him down. Taeyang laughed shaking his head. "Pathetic," he thought before patting his friend's shoulder. Heechul let out a sigh in defeat. Autumn came up to them, her eyes sparkled, the aura around her pulsed with a childlike joy that caused Taeyang to smile at her in response.

"Was it that bad, Heechul?" she asked trying not to laugh her socks off, he looked so defeated.

Heechul dramatically fell to his knees cursing his luck at her question. Fate had been so utterly cruel. Not one single number. It was such a blow to his pride.

Autumn and Taeyang exchanged looks before laughing. Their friend's wallowing was amusing but it was starting to attract stares from the people around them after a couple of minutes. Giving each other a quick nod, they lifted Heechul up from the floor. He was surprisingly light for someone who was almost six feet tall.

The day overall, was the best that Autumn had the pleasure of experiencing in this country thus far.

"We're going," Taeyang said curtly before walking off.

He was tired and they had seen every inch of this museum already.

Autumn and Heechul followed, giggling behind him as they did. They left the museum, heading off to Taeyang's brother's house except for Heechul who decided to go to a local bar to chill out and recover from his latest romantic defeat.

Taeyang's brother greeted them with a bow. Autumn was pleasantly surprised and returned the gesture. His sibling was quite attractive she noticed, as she looked him up and down.

"I'm, Jung-Hwa," he introduced himself in English to Autumn who smiled.

The first thing she noticed was the smell of the ocean breeze mixed with a woodland pine scent that wafted from him. Jung-Hwa had a deep tan, his black hair was wavy, and grown out, almost touching his shoulders. His eyes were a deep blue that swirled with wisp of green. Jung-Hwa was a tad shorter than Taeyang, but his smile was winsome, that left her feeling giddy every time he looked her way. However, Taeyang, and Jung-Hwa were similar in one sense. Both of them hated mess. Jung-Hwa's house was spotless. No dust, no dirt, not even a hair out of place.

The place was interesting. The lack of furniture gave the place a minimalist yet meticulous aesthetic. Autumn felt Taeyang's warm hand clip hers. She blushed; from the minute they had entered the house Taeyang had been hanging around her. He wasn't the clingy type, so his newfound need to be near her space was off-putting. Autumn moved away from him not missing the disappointment that vanished as soon as it appeared on his face. Jung-Hwa put his arm around Autumn's shoulders causing her to blush. Taeyang on the other hand, grinned, a tinge of anger sparkling in his eyes, pushing through them as he sauntered off to the kitchen. Autumn shot daggers at his back before smiling sweetly at Jung-Hwa.

Autumn looked out of the window, watching as children played on the rocks. This island had a mystical ethos about it. The shimmer of the dark brown rocks, along with the crystal blue waters and white sands made her feel as if she was on a different planet. If her deadline wasn't coming up, she would have twisted Taeyang's arm to stay a couple more days. A knock at the door reined her mind back into reality. She advanced to the door before unlocking it. Standing there with a pleasant smile on his face was Jung-Hwa, her face lit up before letting him inside.

"Is your room, okay?" Jung-Hwa asked as he stepped in.

Autumn tapped her chin for a minute, humming.

"Hm, well...nah of course, it's okay friend," she cooed.

Jung-Hwa exhaled looking relieved. She noted his sanguine cheeks and his shaky breath but decided to let him be.

"That reminds me, your English is great. I meant to mention it earlier, but I got kind of side-tracked," she said looking at her feet. Jung-Hwa laughed.

"Thanks, I spent a couple of years overseas when I was in college," he told her.

"Ah, where did you go?" Autumn enquired, she hoped that he would say Canada since most people go to the states to study.

"America, it was a wild trip," Jung-Hwa responded.

She sighed. Jung-Hwa perched himself on the freshly made bed.

"My brother can be a difficult man. I'm sorry for his actions, please excuse him," he told her.

Autumn waved it off. "Taeyang is a great person, he's kind, compassionate in his own way but every time he opens up, he closes down just as quickly," she informed him.

Jung-Hwa nodded.

"I understand that. But don't be discouraged, he will come through just give him time," he assured her before getting up.

She nodded, trying not to yawn, her body felt tired.

Jung-Hwa looked at her thoughtfully.

"Do you want some dinner?" Jung-Hwa asked.

She shook her head. "Thanks, but I don't have much of an appetite right now," she said giving him a small smile.

Jung-Hwa shook his head. "I insist, you've been walking around all day, and I made a special dish. Jeju Black Pork. It would make me happy if you did," he chimed, giving her the most adorable look possible.

She sighed, conceding defeat. It was the least she could do since he had gone through so much effort.

"Alright, if it makes you happy then I'll be happy to do it," Autumn responded.

Jung-Hwa messed with her hair before departing to go and congratulate his rather stubborn sibling on his latest single. Autumn tittered, trying not to blush. Jung-Hwa was silly but charming in his own way. He was a complete extrovert compared to Taeyang who basked in his own company when he wasn't expected to be Mr perfect idol. Jung-Hwa on the other hand, works as a marine biologist on the island. It turns out that he has helped to clean up the ocean and has managed to save the local turtle population from going extinct. The locals speak highly of him. Autumn laughed fighting off a blush before she went off to the bathroom to take a nice rejuvenating bath. Today had been really fun.

Taeyang rushed into the bathroom unzipping his pants pushing them down as his bladder begged for sweet relief.

Suds, water, and clothes went flying in an instant.

Autumn screamed her lungs out, "TAEYANG!!!"

This caused Taeyang to fall back with his trousers and boxers half-way down. Autumn scrambled trying to grab a towel and potentially a shampoo for her eyes.

Taeyang caught a glimpse of her full naked body. It was a glorious blend of muscle and perfectly tanned skin. Each ripple of her body was like a delicate feather on an angel's wing moving rhythmically. A heavy sponge hitting his face brought him back to reality whilst stinging his eyes. He coughed hard pushing his inner monologue to the back of his mind as he suddenly remembered that he still had his trousers down and his friend was poking out. He kept his back to her feeling utterly exposed. He scrambled to his feet pulling up his boxers and trousers. A blush ever-present on his face as he did so.

The vinyl floor was drenched with watery suds, and to Taeyang's chagrin, so were his new brown flip flops. Autumn stood there frozen, pressing a red towel against her dripping wet body as she stared at him. Her mouth moved but only a squeak emanated from her. Taeyang felt heat pool at the bottom of his gut. He had seen her naked body. One that he knew will haunt his dreams for the rest of his life. Every instinct in his system erupted, and it took each grain of willpower that he possessed for him to leave without going over to Autumn and kissing every part of her beautiful self over until she looked as red as her towel. This in itself created more turmoil within his already cloudy thoughts.

"What is Autumn to me?" Taeyang asked himself, breathing heavily.

If he were honest, in the short time he had gotten to know her, she had infuriated him, at one point he had hated her yet he'd grown incredibly attached to her recently. She brought a spark back into his life that he never knew had faded. On top of the sasaengs harassing him, he struggled at being anything but a leader, an image for his company. Taeyang checked himself over, he grumbled at what he saw below his waist. He definitely needed a cold shower now.

———◆◇◆———

Chapter Seven

Drowning In Conflict

Taeyang sat at his brother's kitchen table shifting in his wooden chair when Autumn entered the room. Tension coated the air. Taeyang refused to look at Autumn, after what had transpired in the bathroom, and she was embarrassed that he had seen her in such a vulnerable position but also annoyed at him for not knocking first. She stepped over to the fridge, sifting through the contents. She pulled out a bottle of water before sitting down in the chair farthest away from him.

He observed her, she seemed to be just as embarrassed about the whole ordeal as he was.

"This is ridiculous, I'm an idol, she should be the one saying sorry for not locking the door or putting up a sign," he told himself before getting up and snatching her bottle.

"H-hey, just wait a minute-" Autumn protested but was interrupted by Taeyang who put his hand up in front of her.

She bit her tongue trying to repress the urge to hit him. He was acting like an ass. She glared at him as he took slow and deliberate gulps of her water.

Autumn's stomach growled eliciting a laugh from Taeyang.

"What is it, what's so funny?" she asked Taeyang who lobbed the empty bottle at her.

She easily deflected it. Her anger growing towards his current attitude. After all he was the one in the wrong here.

"I'm just surprised that you are as famished as you are since you ate so much at the museum," he remarked causing her to stand, her lips slightly pulled back.

"Real mature Taeyang," she retorted as she clenched her teeth.

"Real mature Taeyang. Look at me, I'm Autumn and I don't know how to lock a door," he mocked her.

"At least I know how to knock Taeyang. Or is it beneath you to do so?" Autumn asked giving him a dirty look.

"No but this conversation is and if you're not going to apologise then don't talk to me," Taeyang snapped at her.

Deep down he knew that he was being a jerk. But he couldn't help it. The feelings that Autumn's body had stirred within him. They were overwhelming. Intoxicating. If he wasn't attracted to her before, he sure as hell was now. It worried him, what if he lost control and gave into his desires? Then things would become even more complicated. If that were even possible at this point.

Dinner was a tense situation among the three. Jung-Hwa looked between Autumn and Taeyang who kept shooting daggers at each other.

He had no idea what had transpired between the two but he could guess that somehow his brother had either started it or had somehow made it worse.

"Ready to apologise?" Taeyang asked between bites.

"For what? You walked in on me!" Autumn protested.

"Tch! Wrong answer," he responded.

Taeyang stood up pushing his plate away and was about to leave when Autumn called him out.

"Hey! Aren't you going to at least say thank you for the food? Your brother has made an effort for us!"

He rolled his eyes dramatically at that before responding

"Before you met me, you barely understood Korean customs. Now, you have the nerve to lecture me about them? Pathetic," he stuck his nose up at her.

She flinched back; his words were a blow to her already shaky resolve.

"Says the man who thinks Canada is some strange foreign land out of a story book," Autumn muttered before stabbing her fork into a piece of well-cooked pork.

"What was that?" Taeyang asked, knowing exactly what she said.

"Nothing. Absolutely nothing," she remarked as a saddened look came over her.

Taeyang turned his head away before leaving with an air of arrogance in each step. Jung-Hwa sat watching the exchange. He wanted to punch some sense into Taeyang.

The door opened; grubby yellow light peeked into the room from the hallway, before the door was closed over. A dark figure tiptoed across the floor; a breeze cascaded across the room from the open window creating a chill. The room was still except for the occasional squeak from the floorboards. The figure pulled something out of their pocket. The glow that the moonlight outside cast upon the room made the object shimmer and revealed part of the person's pale face. It was a girl with straight black hair, and smoky eyeliner on that hung lifelessly over her bloodshot brown eyes. The strange girl edged closer to the bed as Autumn turned in her slumber causing the duvet to slip off onto the floorboards. The girl held the knife above Autumn's head before she drove the knife down in her direction. Autumn shrieked awake as the knife missed her by an inch. She dodged another attempt screaming her lungs out as she did so.

The door crashed open, to Autumn's relief, Taeyang appeared, before tackling the girl to the ground. The girl screamed, scratching and punching at his face. Taeyang easily bested her in strength as he restrained her body. He did his best to hold back his insane fury. If Autumn hadn't been there, he would have inflicted more severe injuries upon this sasaeng.

Heechul followed by Jung-Hwa charged into the room upon hearing screaming and a loud rumble from outside.

"What's going on here?" they demanded furiously in Korean.

But quickly got their answer when they saw Taeyang wrestling with a crazed woman on the floor, a discarded knife near their feet and the outline of Autumn's shaking figure as she cried in the dark.

Jung-Hwa flicked on the bedroom light before rushing towards Autumn as Heechul assisted Taeyang with the stalker fan. Autumn cried profusely as shock and fear put her in an inconsolable state. Jung-Hwa hugged her fiercely as Heechul managed to help get the stalker fan to their feet. Autumn pressed her face into his chest as he rubbed her back gently.

"It's alright, Autumn. Just relax okay. No one is going to harm you," Jung-Hwa whispered gently to her.

Taeyang glanced at the two, jealousy crawled across his veins, pooling into his heart. But a look into her shaky blue orbs was enough to get him to block this feeling. Autumn had almost been murdered in cold blood, she sought comfort in anything and anyone she could in that moment, it wasn't personal. Taeyang exhaled, wrapping an arm around the sasaeng's neck tightly. Part of him was tempted to strangulate it for what she had done but that would just hurt himself and Autumn more. The woman's eyes darted around with saliva dripping down her face from the corner of her mouth. This woman was downright unstable and seemed to be either on drugs or demonically possessed.

Heechul was at the pinnacle of hatred mixed with fear. The sasaeng had a deluded smile across her face, her eyes staring at Taeyang. He growled; he wasn't in the mood to deal with a deranged stalker fan.

Autumn looked up through tears at Taeyang and the stalker fan.

Something inside of her snapped as she saw the womans smile because before she knew what she was doing she pushed herself out of Jung-Hwa's embrace and marched over to this psychotic stranger. She then smacked her hard across the face.

"How-w dare you! You stupid, evil, conniving..." her voice cracked, she started blubbering harder as she went to hit her again.

Taeyang tried to fight a grin as he saw Autumn hit her. If it were up to him, he'd let Autumn go to town on this crazy woman but there were laws and unfortunately even these stalker fans had rights. Heechul on the other hand felt sympathy for her. The hurt in her was evident.

She went to smack the woman for a third time who began laughing wildly when Jung-Hwa firmly grabbed her hand.

"Autumn, that's enough. You won't feel better doing this and for all that is good and sacred shut her up," he demanded glaring at Taeyang.

Taeyang covered the stalker's mouth as he and Heechul dragged her out of the room.

The local police took the sasaeng into custody. Dark Star Seven didn't need the publicity right now, so Taeyang agreed to meet the officer's daughter and give her a tour backstage at their next concert in exchange for his silence and discretion. Autumn hadn't said much after speaking to the officer which Taeyang had to translate. He hoped that the sasaeng would be thrown into an institution or the depths of Hell for doing to Autumn what she did. The most disturbing part to him was the sasaeng's reason for what she did.

"If I can't have him, no one will ever have him. Autumn should die for even touching him," she had rambled to the detective.

It turns out that, this sasaeng was one of the duo that had been following Taeyang and co for months on end. Recently they had become sloppy after they had successfully broken into the dorm and stole not only property, but also a kiss from Taeyang whilst he had been sleeping.

"I hope that I didn't catch whatever insanity seems to be infecting these people," he complained, wiping his lips with the back of his hand at the thought.

Taeyang sifted through the pictures, and other evidence the detective had given him. The house had been bad enough but to discover the extent of what had gone on for presumably months maybe even years, laid out like this made certainty wobble. These sasaengs had hired a private detective to find out every detail about Taeyang, and they had plans to hire a group to "take care" of Autumn. What caught him off-guard was seeing the signatures of his manager and Mr Quay. It didn't make sense. Unless Chen faked the signatures. But why would he want to get rid of Autumn?

Autumn lay in bed with dented pillows scattered around her head, tears continued to fall from her eyes as her body lay there. Taeyang stood vigil at the doorway, not sure how to comfort her. No matter how often he tried to push it down, guilt came to the surface. The sasaeng was only there because of him. She was crying now only because of him. He should reach out to her, but he stopped himself. The damage was done, they both had to accept that and move on. He watched her burrow further under the covers before he turned away to leave. Jung-Hwa was leaning against the wall with his arms folded. A frown planted firmly on his handsome features. Taeyang fidgeted with his ring, a frown of his own forming.

"What?" he spat not looking his brother in the eye.

"I was just curious, why do you deny what is so obvious brother?" he asked him.

"I don't know what you are implying but I'm not going in there because she is too upset right now," he retorted trying to control his rising temper.

"Are you sure that's all? It seems like that there is more to it than that," he provoked further, holding back a smile as he lured him snugly into his trap.

Taeyang's brown eyes flashed, but his brother managed to catch a peek of the genuine emotion that lay dormant beneath his stubbornness.

"What's your point, Jung? My business with Autumn has nothing to do with you!" he snapped at his brother giving him a hostile look.

"It may not be, but since you're in my house, I'm making it my business. And my point is that I like Autumn and she's single," Jung-Hwa replied.

"You also like pork belly. Your tastes aren't the best," Taeyang said coolly.

"Autumn is to my taste, so if you don't act on what you obviously feel then I guess that means I can have her. And if you don't soon then I will," he gave him an admonition.

Taeyang grabbed his arm. Tempted to wipe the smirk off his brother's mouth. He knew what he was doing.

"She's not yours," Taeyang seethed holding his arm tight.

"Nor is she yours, brother," Jung-Hwa rebutted as he pushed his arm out of Taeyang's grasp before sauntering off.

Taeyang rolled his eyes before glaring at the banister. Jung-Hwa was right. He seemed to be in these situations more than he would like to be lately, this only adding to his growing irritation. Being here was hard enough for him; his younger sibling resembled their mother in various ways. Even the way in which he spoke at times. Part of him was starting to regret taking this trip. His brother wouldn't let the subject drop, which backed him further into a corner he didn't feel like being in. He then had to contend with the fact that Autumn seemed to find his sibling attractive. This really got under his skin.

Turning around back towards the bedroom door Taeyang peeked through taking a look at Autumn who was still under the covers crying her heart out. His brown eyes softened seeing her in such a state. He took gentle steps towards the bed before he sat down.

"Autumn?" he whispered to her.

She moaned in response.

Sighing he pulled back the white duvet and slid under it beside her. Using his hand, he pushed wet and clumpy strands of brown hair out of her face that was hot, red, and blotchy.

"Autumn. Please don't cry. It's not worth it," Taeyang said to her softly.

"I-I can't…" Autumn responded.

"Shh, I promise you leafy, the woman who attacked you will never come near you again," Taeyang said trying to make his words sound believable.

Taeyang gathered her into his arms. She didn't put up a fight or say anything. She really needed his embrace, after everything she had been through. She needed to feel safe even if it was only for now. Autumn's body untensed in his arms, her tears stained his white sweatshirt making it see-through. But he didn't mind. She was processing copious amounts of trauma, and at least crying was all that she was doing. After all she could be throwing chairs or drowning herself with alcohol right now. Taeyang stroked her head gently as she buried her face into his clean neck trying to escape through his touch. His subtle pine scent lowered her stress as she fell into his calming energy.

Time seemed to stretch on as they cuddled up together. She pulled back an inch. Her blue eyes were puffy and swollen from crying, so she kept her head down.

"Thank you, Taeyang. I know that this stuff makes you uncomfortable," she spoke, her voice hoarse and crackly from crying.

"It's fine Autumn. You've had a rough time. It's normal to feel upset," he said before bopping her warm nose gently.

They spent a little longer in each other's embrace before they decided to go to the beach to destress for a little while.

Autumn stopped dead in her tracks, noticing a moving line of green coming from the beach. Her eyes lit up.

"Turtles!" she exclaimed showing off a toothy grin.

Her heart soared upon seeing the adorable creatures heading into the sea. Their little feet making a long trail of steps within the pale-yellow sands as their green bumpy shells glittered against the rays of the burnt sun. Taeyang looked in the direction that she was getting excited over. In the dusty sands were a row of baby turtles heading towards the sea.

"I don't understand it. That turtle is weak, why wait for it?" he commented noticing that one smaller turtle was struggling to keep up with the others.

Autumn sighed. "You know Taeyang, love and faith transcend every timeline, every chapter, every obstacle, and every reason why it's not meant to be so when it's real, when it's there - nothing can ever really stop it," she told him as they watched the green turtles crawling into the crisp blue water.

"Your point is?" he asked her, causing her to roll her eyes.

"That just because it's weak doesn't mean that it deserves to be left behind. It is trying its best to reach the water. I believe that it will do so," Autumn explained.

He nodded softly as he watched it continue on until it did in fact reach the water. He became transfixed by this wonderous event. Autumn looked to him as he did. Without his stoic expression he looked a lot younger, there were less creases near his mouth and a vagrancy about his brown eyes. For a moment, he wasn't this idol that travelled the world and did cool things but just a man enjoying the simplicity of life. Her eyes sparkled with adoration, as she found herself leaning in closer. He moved forward suddenly causing Autumn to stumble. She fell onto her knees; small stones lodged into her skin causing her to flinch and curse under her breath.

Taeyang turned to her and tried to stifle a laugh before giving her his hand and helping her up. She pulled her hand away once she was up choosing not say anything, her mouth was dry, and her chest tightened. The stones digging into her skin came off leaving tiny red dents on her knees. She turned her attention back to the beach. Autumn's mind was ablaze, she felt slightly embarrassed. "Why did I just do that?" she thought to herself as she looked at the water.

Taeyang put his hand through his hair, looking between her and the beach. He wondered where her mind was, if she was thinking about her home back in Canada. He wouldn't be surprised if she was missing it terribly especially after what has happened to her here.

Autumn shivered, as lovely as her dress was, when it came to keeping her warm – it was totally useless. He noticed her shivering and sighed, removing his thick hoodie before placing it delicately onto Autumn's shoulders. She fought a blush at this action but continued watching the waters until the last turtle had returned home.

Taeyang decided to take a detour with Autumn before going back to his brother's place. He wanted to blindfold her to surprise her, but after her last experience, he didn't want to cause her any fear or bring up that particular memory. He took her small hand within his own. She smiled at this gesture. Taeyang's hands felt softer than before. "He must be using his brother's moisturiser," she thought to herself. Autumn bit her lip turning her head to the side. Taeyang remained oblivious as he tried to recall the path he used to take when he was younger.

Each step made Autumn feel flighty, so she held Taeyang's hand tighter. She expected trouble at this point. After her recent experiences, she grappled with herself, her worldview was wildly different than the one she had come here with. Never in her life did she think that you could be treated so horribly yet loved to such an extreme degree in the same space. A small snap caused her to stiffen up before looking around. Taeyang looked back at her, his arrogant smile faded seeing the fright forming across Autumn's features as her eyes darted around.

"No one's here. But if you are a going to be a chicken about it then we can go back," Taeyang said attempting to tease her.

"No! N-no it's just that..." Autumn spoke although softer this time.

"It's just that, I'm worried that someone might be following us Tae," she confessed, her anxiety on full display as she continued looking around.

Taeyang sighed, before he checked the dense bushes and trees around them - no one else was around. She still didn't seem to be convinced, so he kicked each shrub and bush with his foot to emphasise the fact that they were empty and both of them were indeed alone. Autumn's body visibly untensed at that and her shoulders slumped slightly as she gave him a weak smile. He held her hand, stroking it until she fully relaxed. He knew that their last encounter with those men had really upset her, but he had no idea that it still bothered her to this degree.

Taeyang paused before heading to the right. Part of her wondered if he knew where exactly he was going. Autumn fought off a yawn, her body was starting to catch up with her. Her feet were especially sensitive with each stone, leaf and piece of plant debris she walked across. She could feel her eyes growing heavy as they continued walking. He smirked, watching her for a minute. Autumn slipped into a daydream; she was on a ship sailing across calm crimson waters. The clouds were lavender with a deep purple rouge as a blanket of stars swirled in-between. There was a sunset in the distance that changed between an orange and yellow ochre to a pinkish purple. The ship itself was traditional, wooden, and quite the adorable structure.

Autumn looked at herself as she watched the water and gasped. She was younger. Filled with the joys of spring as she began dancing around the boat singing her heart out. No one else was around. A shimmering orange koi swimming in the water caught her attention as she skipped closer to the edge of the boat. It was moving sporadically until it jumped up and shot water into her face.

Cold water covered her head breaking the spell she had fallen under. Taeyang howled with laughter at Autumn's dripping face. She gave him the nastiest glare that she could summon as she marched over to him wanting to kick his behind. The bottle of water he had pulled out of his pocket now discarded somewhere behind him. Taeyang wiped his eyes before putting his hands up.

"Come on, Autumn. You have to admit that you were out of it and I'm sorry but your expression was hilarious!" he said to her.

"No! And next time I space out, just tap my shoulder like a normal person, you hoser!" she retorted before kicking his ankle.

Taeyang flinched but couldn't stop another round of laughter that erupted from his soul.

As they ventured on farther, they passed an old stone wall lining the trail. It was stupendous how one forest could have such a variety of areas. Autumn stroked her hand against it, touches of moss made the edges softer. Her face and hair had dried out by now and her anger had worn off.

The next area they entered, the trees were spaced out, and a stone bench sat behind one of the trees on the right side of the trail. Autumn's foot clipped against something hard. Next to her foot was a pile of cloud grey rocks. Taeyang laughed at that, trust Autumn to knock something over. They then continued on.

They pushed past overgrowth, low hanging branches, and such, before a space finally opened up. Both of them stopped catching their breath as they observed the area around them. Taeyang looked over to Autumn and noticed a green object sticking out of her hair.

He extracted a small leaf from Autumn's brown locks.

"T-thank you," she said, her composure melting under the softness of his touch.

It was fleeting but she felt a spark when he touched her.

"You're welcome, leafy," he said holding back a laugh at the irony.

A gentle fondness came across his face as he moved his hand to touch her cheek. Sparks zapped across her skin making her eyes dilate as she stared into Taeyang's shimmering ones that were like semi-sweet chocolate melting into her soul. He was a two-sided coin. One that had never failed to either dazzle or anger her so far.

The place that they were in resembled a setting straight out of a child's story book. The greens were luscious lime, the air was a melody of scents, with cherry flowers. A sprinkle of mist covered the trees adding to its mystical allure. Autumn felt like one of her protagonists. A plethora of novel ideas flowed into her mind with each rattle of the leaves.

Taeyang caught Autumn off guard when he extracted his hand from her cheek and started to speak.

"I discovered this place when I was a kid. My brother and I had gone exploring,"

Autumn curled her lips back. "So how did you discover it?" she asked, looking around.

Taeyang pushed a loose brown hair back behind her ear causing her to blush, before answering. "Well, I got bored, and decided to go off from the main path. I kept travelling onward until I tripped over a loose log. Nah, just kidding. I stumbled across this place after having a race with my brother. One that I won by the way,"

She whacked him in the chest causing him to cough.

"Idiot," she scolded in her head. He could be such a pain sometimes but it was nice to see him open up.

He flicked her ear before jogging ahead.

Autumn made a face at him and a noise of discontent before following his lead.

They arrived at an intimate clearing, Taeyang slowed his pace as they walked through the entrance. Autumn leaned on one foot stretching up to touch a flower that had caught her eye. The tranquillity of this place made the anxiety crawl right out of her body. Her fingertips touched the pinkish soft petal causing a warm chill to skip down her vertebrae. She giggled; her joy broke through her composure as she started skipping around. Taeyang observed her antics. The way her dress and body synchronised as she danced around the emerald grass. The white dress that she wore matched the flowers and vines around her well. She bore the resemblance of a guardian angel or a goddess. Her beauty could not be compared to the ordinary world around her. She paused in her movements feeling the intensity of his stare. He just smiled and nodded to her as she smiled back.

Taeyang sat cross-legged doing a bit of meditation. He seemed at peace for once. Autumn started humming as she traced each flower with her fingers. This place was romantic. A perfect picnic spot. "Maybe I can convince him to come back here for a picnic once this is all over," she thought to herself before taking another step. There were papilio dehaanii butterflies flying around them, a couple chasing each other, but a few were scattered across different flowers, savouring each one.

Images of a little mischievous Taeyang running around here and causing lots of trouble made her laugh wholeheartedly as she watched the butterflies. Thinking on it, she wondered why Jung-Hwa and his relationship was strained. His brother seemed like a great guy. "Maybe it's something to do with his mother," she thought to herself. All roads seemed to lead back to her somehow. It was rather sad.

"He's so stubborn, even if I asked, he'd probably make up an excuse," Autumn drawled under her breath placing her chin on her hand.

A twig hitting her back caused her to turn around and face him. She noticed Taeyang putting his hand down and using it to pat the short grass beside him giving her an expectant look. She deflected the next twig with her arm, before raising an eyebrow at Taeyang.

"And just what was that for eh?" she asked him before folding her arms.

He shrugged. "I just wanted to," he stated, a smirk formed as he noticed her pouting.

She walked over before plopping down next to him, he was being annoying.

"If you aren't careful, leafy, you are going to be stuck like that," he teased before adding,

"Forever," whilst wriggling his fingers in the air mockingly.

She tipped her head back letting out a groan of indignance. Taeyang could be such a brat at times.

There was a calm silence between the two for a while until Taeyang spoke up.

"What was your childhood like, Autumn?"

She looked between the tops of the trees, her eyes darkening into pools of ice before responding. "My childhood was good in the beginning despite my father's issues and then after my father died...I... was handed over to my older cousin. He wasn't a good man, he got a kick out of humiliating me, insulting me, and starving me when I refused to participate in his mind games,"

Taeyang clenched the grass in his hand upon hearing that.

"Why?" Taeyang rasped, trying to control his rising anger,

She sighed. "That was his idea of entertainment. I wasn't the only one that he did that to, but I got the worst of it because I was family," she informed him shifting uncomfortably as her memories played out in her mind.

"So, what happened after that?" Taeyang pressed on as he plucked out a blade of grass.

Autumn inhaled deeply before continuing. "I left home at fifteen, I managed to get a job as a store clerk then once I turned nineteen, I submitted my manuscript, gained an agent and was signed with a book publisher,"

Taeyang looked at her in awe and in sadness. She had gone through so much yet had managed to come out the other side, without being bitter or jaded. For that, he had to admit that he did respect her.

"That must have been difficult. Did you even go to school?" he delved deeper.

She shook her head. "At that point, I didn't think of education, I wanted to be free, so I just worked," she said smiling.

Taeyang mused over her words for a moment before asking another barrage of questions.

"So, how did you rent an apartment? And survive? And when did you have time to write?"

She shook her head laughing. "Quit interrogating me, I know that my life story is so fascinating, but patience is a virtue. Anyway, to answer your questions, I gave the landlord a fake ID, the dumbass didn't see past it since I had.... matured by then," she revealed before biting her lip and looking away.

Taeyang made a disgusted face at that.

But Autumn continued. "As far as surviving goes, I know how to cook, clean, pay bills, and take care of myself since my cousin was a man-child who made me do everything. And on the weekends, I wrote since I didn't work on those two days,"

Taeyang was speechless, a newfound respect that had cocooned in his chest now emerged into a beautiful new emotion that made him feel at peace. She really was incredible.

Now it was Autumn's turn to ask him questions.

"So, what about yourself? How did you go from island boy to K-pop idol?"

A touch of pink highlighted his cheeks at that last part.

Taeyang cleared his throat before responding, "Well, that's complicated, it would take a million lifetimes to tell you."

She scoffed. "No, it won't, so spill," she retorted looking at him.

He poked her shoulder. "You're annoying." he moaned, but Autumn poked him back.

"And you're an asshole. Answer the question, unless you are a geobjaeng-i," Autumn baited grinning at the horrified look that came over Taeyang's face.

"How dare you! A coward wouldn't have saved your ass so many times, and you have the nerve to call me, one of Korea's most successful men, a coward. Hmph!" Taeyang ranted folding his arms.

Autumn laughed hard seeing a little pout develop across his face as he stared at a brown-eared bulbul perching on a tree. After a few minutes Autumn calmed down enough to talk.

"Look, I'm sorry but your face was priceless. I'll stop if you agree to tell me, eh?" wiping the tears from her eyes, her sweet smile never left her reddened face.

Taeyang gave her a dirty look thinking over her proposal before lying back down.

"Well, my journey as an idol began after my father passed on." Taeyang sucked in a breath fighting back the nausea as he spoke.

Autumn stroked his hand with her own.

"It's okay if you don't want to go into it, I won't force you," she whispered.

Taeyang composed himself, before going on.

"My father worked many hours and was gone a lot. My mother became lonely and started seeing another man. Eventually my father found out and disowned her. The shame of it caused her to commit suicide. My father eventually followed,"

Autumn put her hand over his, as her eyes watered.

"Goodness Tae, that is truly awful. I'm so sorry that happened," she sympathised.

"Thanks Autumn, but it was a long time ago, I'm okay now so don't get upset," he reassured her before wiping her eyes with his thumb.

He continued, "Well, once the funeral had occurred, my younger brother along with myself were sent to live with our uncle. He was a fisherman but back in the day he worked as a professional pianist for an entertainment company. It was a sunny day when it happened, the radio blared, I just had a banana milk."

"Taeyang, I want a story not a blow-by-blow description of the scenery, what you drank, or the porch," she interjected.

Taeyang covered her mouth playfully before continuing.

"As I was SAYING, he heard me singing on the porch and handed me a flyer. It was for rookie auditions in Seoul, and well I tried out for it,"

Autumn listened intently, her brow creased for a moment.

"Why did your uncle have the flyer?" she asked.

Taeyang shrugged, sitting up.

"I'm not sure, it was in the mail probably," he assumed.

Autumn let her mind wander before Taeyang continued speaking.

"I was selected by the company, and then sent to live at the trainee dorms. Every day we trained. We had acting lessons, singing lessons, Chinese lessons, English lessons and dance practice. At first, I wanted to go home, my body felt so beaten up by the end of each day,"

She grasped at her heart upon hearing that.

"That sounds awful. How did you endure that for such a long stretch of time?" she asked, concern building in her throat.

"It's worth enduring pain for the love of something. I fell in love with music. I could imagine myself on the stage but nowhere else, it became a second home for me. The worst part of it was stuff like the weigh-ins, not being able to see my uncle or my brother. But those were the rules, and the trainee contract was signed by my uncle, so I had no say," he admitted.

"You could have left," she pointed out.

"You could have stayed, and waited until you were eighteen," Taeyang countered giving her a knowing look.

"But you didn't and neither did I because we both saw what was necessary and did it," he said staring into her eyes.

This stunned her. He seemed sincere in his admission.

"A couple of years in, we had a few members enter and leave the group. There was one kid, Kim, who had been kicked out of his old company for getting another trainee pregnant. It was a scandal, and I had to practically beg the CEOs to take him on but they did under the condition that if he screwed up, then I would take full and personal responsibility. We ended up forming Dark Star Seven and our debut album was a number one for weeks on end. We toured everywhere but after so many years without contact, I grew apart from my brother and uncle," Taeyang recalled staring at her briefly before going on.

"There was a rookie I was close to, but I changed companies, so we lost touch. But as an idol my priorities have been my band, and my fans. There are rules about dating at the company,"

"Like what?" Autumn wondered out loud.

"Well, we can't date before debut and even after debut we need to wait several years but the rules vary from company to company," Taeyang enlightened her.

She scratched her ear that a blade of grass was tickling before piping up,

"Do they at least have a reason for such a policy?"

"Supposedly, it's so that we don't get distracted, but I think it's because we are more attractive if we appear attainable," Taeyang said, his eyes clouded over at that.

He tried not to think about himself as a product but when he thought about the way in which he was treated by people it really was hard not to see himself that way.

"So, why did Kim get chosen in that case? It would've been easier to choose another rookie," she commented.

"Well, Kim is a brilliant dancer, and I just liked him. He was able to handle all of the things that I made him endure when we were training, and he never complained. But the company were the hardest on him because of his past," Taeyang said, a tinge of guilt formed in his russet eyes.

Autumn looked at him sadly.

"It's a shame, but mistakes are not something to be marked by but to be learnt from. I'm glad it worked out, at least," Autumn said to him.

Taeyang turned to her smiling.

"So, is there anything else that you want to know?" he asked her.

Autumn thought about his question for a moment before her eyes lit up.

"Why is your hair blue?" Autumn asked him as she flicked his hair.

He swatted her hand away playfully before answering.

"I enjoy space, and the ocean so I chose to dye my hair blue. Plus, it suits me so,"

She mused.

"Ah, so that's why you are so cold and untouchable, oppa," she teased, ruffling his hair.

He hated that word with a passion. Oppa a.k.a older brother, it made him want to puke.

"What have I said before about the hair?" Taeyang warned giving her a playful look.

Autumn shrugged her shoulders, a mischievous grin dabbling on her lips as she decided to test her luck.

"But oppa! I weally wike your hair," she said in a mocking manner causing him to narrow his eyes.

"Don't call me that, leafy, it's just wrong coming from your mouth. And stop acting so childish," he retorted, covering her mouth as she tried to say that word again.

She smirked wickedly before licking his hand.

He retracted it quickly before glaring at her.

"I suppose you'd know all about that," she said before giggling.

"I don't know what you mean," he spluttered trying to regain his composure but failed in epic proportions.

"Whatever you say, oppa," she said, emphasizing the last part.

Then just like that, it was all over. Before she knew what had hit her. Taeyang had tackled her. Autumn oofed as she fell down with him. He positioned himself on top of her. He tickled her neck making her laugh and squirm away, he didn't relent however as he wriggled closer attacking her shoulders and ribcage. She kicked and rolled around pushing and hitting at his hands and chest.

"Quit it!" she shrieked happily.

His competitive side started to make itself known as their clothes collected grass stains and a few stray twigs. Pollen filling both of their senses as the breeze flowed around them. They continued on with their horseplay for a few minutes before they were out of breath and laughing like demented hyenas. They settled into a comfortable afterglow as their breathing returned to normal. Autumn's placid state was like ambrosia as her skin sparkled against the dark green tints of the grass under her head. At this angle, Taeyang was able to see her in a different light. One that pulled him in with ease.

Taeyang leaned forward and kissed her cheek. His mouth felt delicate against her supple skin.

He quickly pulled back once he realised what he was doing,

"You had something on your cheek. It's gone now," he told her trying to avoid her gaze.

His hot breath created goosebumps on her face.

Autumn was tempted to bite his nose as payback for his little stunt. The only thing that prevented her from doing so was the look in his eyes. A vulnerability, almost innocent, glimmered as briefly as the trees baring their fragile leaves in fall.

"So yeah, our group became Dark Star Seven, we debuted, and after four best-selling albums, not including a few singles, and unit eps, we became Korea's top boy band," he gushed out.

She sat there absorbing the information he had told her. They looked at each other before bursting into a fit of giggles. Autumn was enthralled by each part. It left her with a bizarre thirst for more information about his life. Even when he talked about banana milk, she found herself wondering about the brand, the consistency, whether he liked it chilled or room temperature or if he used a straw. She was pulled from her thoughts when he pulled her hair.

"Hey!" she screeched at Taeyang.

"Aw, is leafy getting angry?" he teased, grinning at her.

She scrunched up her face putting her forefinger and thumb close together as she went on,

"Ooh you little..."

He latched his hand onto hers shaking it side to side causing her to laugh. His heart was nagging him to tell her the truth about the manuscript. He licked his parched lips about to speak when the words died in his throat at the look in her blue eyes. Alluring. Seductive. But also, cheeky and so loving.

Taeyang leaned in closer trying to get his breathing under control. He didn't want to scare her off, but the way she looked into his brown eyes told him that she yearned for this as much as he did. Their lips were an inch apart when his phone went off causing them to jump apart. Autumn touched her lips with her fingers too stunned to speak. Taeyang answered the phone before quickly standing up. He walked to the edge of the clearing, and Autumn could tell by the gradual fall of his shoulders that whatever he was talking about made him feel deflated. She twirled the sharp grass with her fingers still trying to process what had just happened. "Was he really going to kiss me? Does that mean?" she asked herself in her mind before shaking her head.

Changing gears. Autumn instead chose to think about the conversation that they had, she counted how many new things she had learned about him. He had his scars, yet he had a playful side that didn't make an appearance much. Which reminded her that they had to get banana milk at some point – it sounded lovely. Watching him she noticed his shoulders tensing sporadically as he paced the grass-stress radiated from him.

"We should go," Taeyang said to her before making a head start out of the clearing barely giving her a second glance.

Autumn kicked the grass as she stood up and followed him.

Taeyang didn't even look towards Autumn as they ventured back. His phone became the most interesting thing ever it seems. The sky had grown considerably saddened with rain clouds floating over their heads which added to her fizzling mood. "Oh Taeyang, why did that phone have to ring?" she thought sadly, her feelings welling up within her chest constraining her ability to speak. He didn't glance back once, even when she tripped over a vine that was poking out. They made it back to Jung-Hwa's house; the front door was ajar which struck them as odd. He stuck his arm out.

"Wait here, leafy," Taeyang spoke as his hair stood on edge.

Something wasn't right. His brother never left the door open.

Autumn tingled at the nickname; it was such a simple term of endearment, yet it made her feel safe and valued. But he had been a jerk, so she pushed his arm aside and sprinted past him. He smirked, his awkwardness temporarily forgotten as he caught up to her and tackled her causing them to burst into laughter as he wrapped her in a bear hug restraining her movements.

Chapter Eight

An Amber Light Ahead

A woman sat there sipping on an ice matcha from a China cup. She looked eloquent; her ginger hair flowed perfectly against the smooth summer breeze. Autumn paused looking to Taeyang who was staring directly at the woman. She was everything that Autumn wasn't; rich, affluent, beautiful and sophisticated. But it was his reaction that had truly unnerved her. He looked at this woman with longing, his chestnut eyes sparkled in a way that uncovered every unspoken word his heart was dying to say to her, and she noted a hint of lust in it too. Autumn wasn't one to be possessive or overly protective, but her gut twisted into a tight knot when she saw the way he hugged this woman. Maybe she was overthinking things but the way that he gripped her back brought a dampness over Autumn's usually upbeat demeanour.

Amber was in the area and had decided to pay Taeyang's brother a visit. Well, that's what she claimed anyway. "I don't trust her," Autumn thought to herself as she watched Amber and Taeyang catch up. Autumn sat there with her hand against her face on the couch. Jung-Hwa gave her a sympathetic look from where he was sitting. From the moment he had seen Amber, Taeyang had disregarded Autumn, and focused solely on Amber, a former trainee from his company. She worked as a model, and an actress nowadays. Taeyang laughed, even snorting in the process. Amber giggled touching his forearm. Autumn clenched her teeth at that, trying to push down images of Amber being hit by a double-decker bus.

Heechul entered the room breaking Autumn's thoughts.

"Taeyang, don't forget that we need to leave soon," he informed them.

Autumn looked up, she had heard enough Korean over the last few days to pick up bits and pieces. So, she used this as an opportunity to leave the room.

"Yeah, well before we go, I'm going to go sort some stuff out," she spoke flatly before getting off the couch.

Taeyang just grunted in response barely noticing her. She brushed past Heechul, her movements held no emotion which surprised both Jung-Hwa, and Heechul who turned towards Taeyang giving him a puzzled glance. He was still preoccupied, too absorbed in his conversation to fully register her shift in attitude. There was no smile. No tenderness. Just a hollow set of words with no meaning or emotion attached to them.

Autumn changed out of her sticky soiled clothes into a fresh set of denim shorts and a light brown baggy t-shirt that was kindly provided by Jung-Hwa. She huffed; her muscles kept cramping; her mindset had descended into utter misery, and she still had no manuscript. She watched her reflection in the mirror. She was pensive, discreetly judging every flaw that existed on her face. She wasn't insecure about her looks normally; they never made a point in her mind yet her feelings for Taeyang were creating a commotion within her set of principles and beliefs that she held about herself. She deadpanned noticing how scruffy her hair was, the tangles and knots bugged her, so she searched for a comb to at least flatten them out.

Taeyang couldn't understand why Autumn was being so hostile. It was a total eclipse from her regular upbeat, gregarious self. Amber was a welcome distraction. What had happened in the woods, it stirred up unfamiliar feelings within his heart. Love was plausible but not practical for the circumstances. He was an idol and lived in completely different part of the world. Amber touched his hand again. He hadn't even noticed that Autumn had left the room until he received a firm tap to the shoulder. Turning to face whoever had disturbed him, he was surprised to see his brother standing there gesturing for him to go after her. Considering the conversation that had transpired between them before. He assumed that he would be the first one to take advantage of this but he didn't.

Amber was straightforward, she was Korean, she lived in Seoul and was strong enough to defend herself. Plus, he was attracted to Amber, but it was a different kind of desirability. A rekindling of the familiar. Taeyang needed to talk to Autumn, if he didn't confront her now then he might never get the chance to, again. Each stair felt like hot coals digging deeper into his brown flip flops, and for the first time in a long time he felt uncertainty.

As he stood in the hallway of the second floor, a memory resurfaced. Taeyang was a lot younger, and he'd just done his first live performance. Amber hid in his dressing room waiting for him to arrive back. From the minute he stepped into the room she was on him. Enveloping him in a hug which caught him off-guard. Neither of them were touchy feely types of people so there must have been good news, or she had overdone it with the caffeine pills again.

"Amber, what's up?" he asked stroking her short locks of fire.

Looking into his russet eyes, her face softened but still held a raring enthusiasm.

"I have a gig overseas. It's a small part in a movie. We're departing tonight," she all but shrilled as she told him.

Taeyang's face fell at that. He nudged her off as he proceeded to sit at his table. Her smile still remained but her confusion was multiplying by the second.

"What's up with you? You seemed fine a minute ago," she asked him.

"It's nothing Amber, just leave me alone," he retorted.

"Why? Why are you being so cold? You're supposed to be happy for me.... but you're just awful and I never want to see you again!" she yelled before slapping him across the face.

Amber ran out of the room in tears.

The hand mark on his face glowed red against his mistletoe berry skin. Gritting his teeth, he whacked his hands against the table. Someone touching his shoulder made him look up. It was his manager; Chen shook his head before turning the boy around to face him.

"Girls are nothing but a distraction. Don't waste your time on them," he had told him firmly.

So, Taeyang didn't, he never chased after her. He erased her number, deleted every picture of her, under his manager's instructions and never thought twice about it until today. Seeing her again reminded him of how selfish he had acted and just how much his success has truly cost him.

That day will always bother him. He was a stupid, and selfish kid back then. He didn't want to repeat his failings with Autumn. Seeing Amber today reminded him of that. Autumn's mere existence created chaos in the chamber of his being, it was a complete contrast to Amber who quelled any ripples within his mind. Yet, the passion he felt around Autumn made the irksome elements of her tolerable. Taeyang arrived at the bedroom door which was open. A light breeze was coming through the room from the open window. The vibe in the room was a stark contrast to that lightness, the hair on his neck stood on edge. At the table, sat Autumn, a couple of scraps of defiled paper building up next to her arm, as she wrote furiously.

Autumn fumbled with her the pen in her hands trying to figure out how to say goodbye to Taeyang. They were going to the mainland, and Autumn wanted a clear head before leaving. She still had to figure out how to tell her agent that she had no manuscript. "That's going to be fun," she thought miserably. Autumn twisted the copper pen within her hand, its cold surface sent a buzz into her heart that made it beat erratically.

She had wasted enough time here, and Autumn still had a job to do after all. She was a bestselling author who had achieved more in her career than many could ever dream of in a lifetime. She had no time for games, distractions or fanciful dalliances that would ultimately break her heart. Her eyes watered several times as she gripped the pen harder within her hand; it was difficult for her to explain how she felt. Taeyang was infuriating. His complexities made her crazy, she wasn't an easily swayed or romantic person.

Men were cute, some more so than others, but none of them had ever caused her to feel such blistering yet compelling emotions before. He could draw her thoughts to the surface, there wasn't anything that he didn't see past. It was strange, but it also came with vices like those crazy fangirls and lavish amounts of constant attention he received. She didn't know how she could fit into his life with all the interviews, meetings, tours, promos, and all the other fanfare. She hated the idea of being his clingy girlfriend who constantly must battle scandals, fans, and whatever else would be thrown at her. Considering how introverted and emotionally constipated he could be at times she was surprised that he loved the spotlight at all.

Taeyang entered the room, closing the door behind him before locking it.

"Autumn, we need to talk," he told her.

Autumn tucked her letter away before standing.

"I think that's first thing we've truly agreed on since this whole thing started," Autumn replied before going over to the bed and perching on it.

He rubbed the back of his neck before joining her.

"What happened in the woods. It was inappropriate, I shouldn't have kissed your cheek or tried to go further. I have obligations Autumn; a relationship would complicate them," Taeyang explained avoiding eye contact.

If he looked into her eyes, he'd be a goner.

Autumn felt a stab of pain at that, his monotone way of speaking wasn't helping her either.

"Right, well you are not the only one who has thought about this situation. I may not be as known as you are, but my career is important to me. Nothing can get in the way of that," Autumn spoke, clutching the duvet.

Taeyang remained zoned out for a minute, her words seemed disingenuous to him. She was the kind of woman who held onto things tightly, who fought for what she cared about so why she was giving him up so easily?" Taeyang introspected, feeling somewhat hurt by this action.

"Whatever this was, it's over Autumn. Please don't contact me again after this," Taeyang requested, pushing down the nausea that was rising within his throat.

Autumn reeled back at this as if he had spewed quark-gluon plasma on her, she expected Taeyang to put his career first, and that was fair but tossing her out of his life as if she were a speck of dirt on his sneakers was not. Her emotions began bubbling up.

"How can you even say that? I may not be Amber, but I do care about you, and for you to do this to me so easily, makes me wonder if you cared at all," she spoke, her voice reduced to a whisper by the end.

He sagged his shoulders forward remaining stoic as he did so but his heart was breaking.

Autumn began to cry and this frustrated him greatly so he grabbed her shoulders and pushed her down onto the bed trying not to hurt her.

"Autumn, do you really think that I'm enjoying this? I'm just trying to be honest with you," he urged gripping her.

The sasaengs are bad now but they'd be extra crazy if they thought that she was his girlfriend. Beyond that, she had a life in Canada. One that was safe and peaceful. In his heart, he knew that she wouldn't have that here. No matter what they did or where they went.

"Y-you can't - like y-you don't even care!" she cried rambling.

Taeyang rolled his eyes at her dramatics. He knew that she wouldn't take it well but seeing her so hurt was making him angry. At himself. At the circumstances. He had to get away from her before his will broke.

"Look Autumn, it's done now. You're going back to Canada. At least I was honest with you. At be grateful for that." he uttered before he extracted himself from her body and the bed.

Autumn sat up in a futile attempt to control her tears. She rose to her feet, her anger spilled over at his words as she found her voice.

"Honest? You think disregarding me like I'm a used piece of clothing, is something to be grateful for? You are just a liar, a stubborn jerk, and so damn proud that you can't see anything else other than yourself! You talk about others but what about you! You ran away from your responsibilities! You lost my manuscript! And on top of that you made me believe that you actually gave a damn about me!" balling her fists as she glared at him.

Taeyang's expression darkened. Her words cut him hard as he turned to the desk and pulled something out of the third drawer before facing her.

"You want to talk about me? Honestly Autumn, you are just an immature weakling! If it weren't for me, you'd be dead in a gutter somewhere or trafficked, maybe try being grateful for the things that I have done, Autumn! I've saved your ass many times at this point! Risked my career and reputation just to keep you safe! Yet you accuse me of not giving a damn. If that's what you believe then here! Take your stupid manuscript! And go back to Canada. See if I care!" he yelled before lobbing her manuscript at her.

Autumn caught her manuscript not fully registering it as she stared at Taeyang. She stood there holding her manuscript as if she had just been burned. Their eyes locked as they both glared at each other. Her chin wobbled as she stared him down. She could feel her body quaking with anger and adrenaline as blood pounded in her ears. Taeyang looked darkly at her before he turned away unlocking the door before slamming it shut as he left. Autumn flinched before she realised something. "Wait! he had my manuscript this whole time?!" she thought angrily as she looked at the bundle in her hands bewildered.

Meanwhile in Seoul, lying on an untidy cream futon was Chen. His head ached, along with his legs. Light seeped through his eyelids that were a crack open. He looked at the letter on his coffee table, there were pictures of Taeyang and Autumn attached to it. Chen growled, throwing his hand down before flinching from the pain penetrating throughout his veins. He held his head; blood chiselled its way around his ears as he felt his blood pressure skyrocketing to new heights. The sasaeng had botched the job and was now in jail. A latest failure in his attempts to restore balance. Chen grasped his phone groaning as he did, if he was going to resolve this issue permanently, he needed to take matters into his own hands.

Taeyang had been unsettled following his argument with Autumn so he decided to visit a private investigator that he had hired to dig up dirt on Chen. The man was the best in South Korea. Best case scenario, everything was just a misunderstanding, but worst-case scenario, there was a conspiracy against himself and anyone else who dared to cross Chen. After a phone call consultation, the detective agreed to meet at Mongle café on the island. He cracked his neck before going in, the stiffness irked him. Depending on the seasons his joints would flare up and became less cooperative. Pain aside, he didn't want to think about Autumn right now.

It was the middle of the night when a knocking came at Autumn's door. She groaned nuzzling deeper into her soft pillows until the knocking became louder and insistent. She huffed before extracting herself from her haven of fluffy pillows. The trudge across the cold floor felt like a never-ending trek across frosty sand dunes but she reached the doorknob within a few seconds. Scratching her neck, she opened the door as the figure before her caused her to blink twice. A drunk Heechul stood there with the light from the hallway illuminating his swaying figure, the liquor on his breath filled her with nausea. He was mumbling whilst giving her a lopsided smile, his cheeks were tinted red, his eyes were dilated, and his shirt had a dark stain on it. Autumn backed up to allow him inside. The look he was giving her becoming more prominent and she became concerned that he might be having a stroke and not actually smiling at her.

"Heechul what are you doing eh? Are you okay?" she asked before giving his face a prompt pinch.

He yelped dramatically before holding his face,

"Ah, so not a stroke then," she deduced as she turned on the bedroom light.

He didn't respond to that but gave her a look that made her step back, the intensity and double meaning it held made her fight or flight senses bristle.

He grunted before pushing past her. She looked up to the ceiling letting out a sigh.

"Heechul?" she asked again, her voice shy as she did so.

He sat on the bed and grumbled something that she didn't understand.

"Are you okay?" Autumn asked.

He grunted before letting out a hoarse whisper,

"I like you. I don't want you to leave again," he turned his head making brief eye contact.

Her ocean orbs became soft, seeing him in such a broken mess made her pity him.

"Blue angel," he croaked out.

Heechul stood up and approached her. He was about to kiss her.

But she didn't like him in that regard.

"Heechul, listen to me. I'm not whoever this blue angel is. You're drunk," Autumn explained pushing a hand against his chest.

He slipped something into her free hand, it was soft and silky. Autumn clasped it in her fingers, a pleasant smell wafted from it. She brought it to her nose inhaling deeply, the smell resembled French pastries and honeysuckles. She looked at it under the bedroom light. The material was a luscious pink silk that had floral patterns across it with depictions of a forest. The smell of alcohol also assaulted her nose as she did her best not to retch as she looked at Heechul. Autumn wasn't a drinker. After her father's experience she figured that it would be better not to tempt fate.

Autumn turned her attention back to the material in her hand. A theory skirted across her mind, given his actions in the past, it was reasonable to assume that his failure with the opposite sex was due to an unresolved rift that he had in his soul. He viewed these women as he would this blue angel person, a woman who was not coming back.

She couldn't begin to understand the kind of grief that it would invoke, people have become insane over less. She wanted to help him but she wasn't sure where to start.

"Heechul, why are you doing this?" she asked him but was silenced when he put his grubby finger against her lips causing her to raise an eyebrow.

His hands were not clean, this made her want to puke, she didn't want to know where they had been last or what they had been doing.

Then he crossed the line as he tried to kiss her,

"Heechul! No!" Autumn shouted, pushing against him.

Taeyang knocked the door off the hinges as he crashed through it, startling both Autumn and Heechul. She stood there frozen for a minute as she dropped the handkerchief before his presence really registered with her. Everything had escalated so rapidly that it caught her still sleepy mind unawares. One minute Heechul and Taeyang were arguing, and the next they were beating the hell out of each other. She wished she had a camera to make sure that this wasn't a twisted nightmare, or a by-product of sleep paralysis. A shoe crashed behind her creating a minor crack on the mirror. Her mouth dropped.

Their private plane had been delayed until tomorrow morning due to a typhoon warning. This meant that they had to stay here tonight. Taeyang had spent the rest of the day reflecting on his argument with Autumn. He felt regret, he didn't want their potentially last interaction to be awful. So, he went to her room to apologise to her when he heard Heechul. At first, he was going to leave but when he heard how drunk Heechul was he decided to listen. That is until he heard Autumn shout. Protectiveness and anger possessed him as he crashed into the room and witnessed his friend trying to kiss Autumn against her will. This caused him to snap.

Taeyang and Heechul started fighting. It wasn't playful, it wasn't fuelled by my blank is bigger than your blank contest that the boys would have occasionally. This was genuine contempt. The epitome of rage between both parties. This horrified Autumn who watched them as they kicked the crap out of each other.

Heechul lunged at Taeyang who seized his arm within his forearms. "Taeyang!" Autumn shouted with tears welling up in her eyes.

But he didn't acknowledge her presence as the fight continued. He landed a particularly brutal punch upon Heechul's shoulder causing the man to cough and groan. But Taeyang was too angered to stop at this point. Heechul had crossed a line. Hearing the fear in Autumn's voice triggered him, it made him want to rip his friend into pieces. Taeyang couldn't stop himself. No Heechul had to pay as they continued to fight.

One particularly hard blow from Heechul sent Taeyang flying. As he hit the ground Taeyang found himself falling into a flashback. The day in question his mind had stumbled back into was the day he got into his first fight. There were a ragtag group of kids in the neighbourhood he grew up in that liked to cause trouble.

Taeyang had been coming home from helping his uncle on the dock when it happened. Since the weather was starting to turn a bit dull and stormy, he decided to take a short cut in order to get home before the storm kicked off. He continued walking until he noticed a random kid sitting in the middle of the road. He slowed his pace, the logical part of his mind pipping up. Why would a kid be unattended? Plus, he didn't seem hurt just confused. The kid appeared to be about seven or eight years of age. There was a pull at his heartstrings as he imagined his baby brother sitting alone, lost and confused. He nodded to himself before advancing to the kid. The second his shoes stopped, the air changed, his body instantly cramping up.

The boy's sad pout twisted into an evil smirk, as random hands yanked the back of Taeyang's shirt. He tried to scream out but a hand covered his mouth. There were a group of young teens there but he didn't get a chance to say anything before the first blow came. Disoriented he pushed himself back up. He managed to bite one of the shorter kids who punched him in the nose before signalling the others to descend. Taeyang couldn't remember the faces of the other boys but he was able to recall the feel of their cold fists and rough sneakers as they used them to beat the crap out of him. He curled up his body and covered his head with his hands clamping his eyes shut. They kicked him before eventually throwing him against a brick wall. As his vision distorted and he heard their nasal little laughs fading farther from his grasp, he internally vowed that he would never go through this again.

Taeyang was pulled back into the present by another punch. He dodged it before he threw Heechul into the desk causing him to fall into a nearby lamp that smashed as it hit the floor. Heechul growled before throwing another punch at him.

"Stop it! Taeyang! Heechul," she shouted as a look of horror marked her face.

Autumn felt anger, fear, and confusion she watched them fight, feeling helpless. As angry as she was at Heechul she felt that Taeyang's reaction was going over the top. Plus, why was he there? She was still reeling after their argument and upset that he had hid her manuscript from her.

Blood spots began staining the floor along with the wall that they had smacked into as well as the desk. She wished that Taeyang's brother was back from the bar already so he could intervene. She ducked out of the way as another lamp went flying, barely missing her head. The room was becoming a demolition zone at this point. This carnage needed to end before permanent mistakes were made or someone actually died.

Autumn grabbed onto a glint of courage as she latched onto Taeyang's arm trying to pull him back, or at least snap some sense into his thick head but it was to no avail. He shrugged her off causing her to wrinkle her face.

"Back off, leafy, this isn't your fight. Get out!" he spat as his jaw muscles rippled.

His tone caused a shiver to crawl up her spine but her rising anger and fear made her continue. Autumn tried again. Taeyang dived forward aiming for Heechul's messy face, but Heechul ducked this time. Autumn put herself between the two causing his hand to smash against her arm. The pain was searing and instant as she yelped and fell to her knees. Anger instantly stripped itself from Taeyang's body, upon seeing her in pain and the sobering realisation that he had caused it. Heechul stood there stunned. The weight of the situation finally dawning on him. He had hit on his friend's potential girlfriend and now had gotten her hurt because he was a drunken stubborn idiot. Guilt ascended his throat as he repressed the urge to be sick.

Autumn held her arm. Trying not to pass out from the pain. She had tears in her blue eyes as she looked at Taeyang who reached down to touch her but she flinched away. Logically, she knew that it was her fault, that she shouldn't have interfered but Autumn assumed that Taeyang would stop once he saw her standing there. "Stupid jerk," she thought miserably before she got back up onto her feet and left the room slamming the door as she did so. Both Taeyang and Heechul were left standing there stunned and feeling guilty as hell.

Heechul's face was bruised, covered in crimson blood with a couple of long cuts decorating his cheekbones and left eyebrow that had started to swell up. Taeyang stared at the door as his hands shook. Replaying the scene in his head a million times. A few nicks and a few bruises marking his strikingly attractive face. Taeyang felt foolish. He had lost control. Had acted like an uncivilised beast. Autumn would probably never forgive him. This made his heart ache as he grasped his chest trying to control his unruly emotions.

Heechul looked around the room, his drunken rage now stoic sobriety as he noticed the mess of broken furniture, shards of glass, drops of drying blood, and the pieces of ripped fabric that decorated the floor. The weight of the damage they had inflicted on each other polluting the air with a thick, and awkward silence. Neither made a move, nor said a word. Taeyang's shirt was stained in streaks with Heechul's blood with a little bit of his own mixed in. Taeyang's chest was heaving up and down as he remained in a trance like state.

"Autumn....I'm sorry," he whispered the baritone velveteen of his voice turned into a meek tremble.

Chapter Nine

Washed Away In Pages Unread

Autumn sprinted down Hamdeok beach as tears flowed freely from her eyes and her shoes crunched against the coarse sand. She wanted to plunge herself within the depths of the unruly sea and never be seen again. Taeyang had hit her. She felt sick. But also, she felt guilt for not listening to him. The rain diminished into random spits of water; each step made her feet curl and spasm but the wretchedness she currently felt outweighed any physical pains including the one currently radiating from her arm. The lingering pain from Taeyang's prior outburst stung at her emotions only adding to her turmoil. "Why did he lose it like that? Why does he feel the need to toy with my heart like this? one minute it's like he doesn't care then the next minute he goes psycho on anyone who hurts me," she agonised inside of her head. Hopelessness filled her to the brim as she looked to the moon that was sitting high above into the quiet night, casting a beam of light upon the sands. The tranquillity of the landscape felt gentle aside from the waters, but it did little to comfort her. Autumn's eyes burned from the salt of her tears that were blurring her sight as she stood near the water's unforgiving edge.

A frosty wave crashed over Autumn throwing off her footing as she fell into the merciless sea. Her screams were drowned out by the salty water rushing into her mouth which she immediately closed. Every passing second felt like a century as she battled against the tyrant that was nature's current. She held her breath breaking through the surface briefly trying to grasp onto some oxygen as the cold wrapped its shackles around her throat. Autumn's body numbed quickly. Her heart growing tired. Awareness fading as she felt her resistance crumbling. Something caught her ankle. Dragging her under the waves. The lack of light made it difficult to see what was dragging her down but she could feel something hard and metallic against her ankle. Panic and adrenaline skimmed across her bones as she started flailing.

Autumn tried to unlatch whatever had caught her ankle but it was steadfast, her body was depleted from the day's events, on top of her aching arm, the cold seeping into her body was making it hard to think. She knew that she only had a couple of minutes to get free before she was in serious trouble. Autumn kicked pushing herself upwards, she wasn't the best swimmer, and the debilitating fear that made its way across every cell of her body didn't help. Salt from the water stung at her eyes making it difficult to see. The air slipped from her lungs as the metallic restraint on her ankle pierced into her skin causing her to open her mouth. Her sight dimmed as her movements became sluggish and uncoordinated. She did her best to fight against the water filling her lungs but it was no use. Her mind drifted to Taeyang, his smile filling her mind as the world went dark around her.

Taeyang, along with Heechul covered the vastness of the beach looking for Autumn. The moon's rays were the only light aside from the yellowish glows that came from the hut windows in the distance. "She has to be somewhere," he thought as he scanned the shoreline. There were a few rocks around. "What if she's hit her head? What if a sasaeng came back to kidnap her?" his thoughts were racing. The protective fondness that he had developed over the last couple of days was roaring to life as he started running to every spot, he imagined that she could be. Heechul checked everywhere that Taeyang missed, but nothing came up. Taeyang noticed markings in the sand that led into the water as he checked another rock. The shoe imprint resembled Autumn's foot size. He signalled to Heechul who jogged over to them.

They looked at the waves before turning to each other fearfully. Taeyang gave a nod before he dived into the dark waters. He kicked and jerked as he coordinated his movements, he swam downward trying to catch a glimpse of Autumn. The pressure became greater as he went further down. His head thumped as water filled his ears, he pushed on further, his lungs tightened with the limited amount of air he had to use.

He quickly spotted Autumn. Her leg was caught in an old hook chain. Taeyang froze for a moment, her body looked so lifeless as it floated. A sudden and very loud ringing inside of his eardrum briskly snapped him out of shock. Taeyang swam over to her as fast as he could and grabbed the rusty chain ripping it from her ankle. Now that she was free, he rushed back to the surface to get help from Heechul. Breaking through the water, he needed help.

"I found her! But I need something to pull us in, Heechul!" He shouted.

As luck would have it, his friend understood him even in his semi sober state and started searching for something to pull them in. Taeyang dived back into the water pushing and fighting against the waves as he made his way back to Autumn.

He rushed back to her and yanked her cold body into his arms gripping her tightly before making his way back to the surface. Heechul had managed to find a rope and tossed it into the water. Taeyang grabbed the rope, clutching Autumn as Heechul pulled them into the shore. Her body remained motionless as he grasped her tightly. Taeyang's nerves were getting shakier by the minute. Her body grew stiffer, this alone sent alarm bells off in his head. "Please Autumn don't die!" Taeyang pleaded in his head as he held her closer.

Once they were back on the beach. Heechul ran over to them getting a better look at Autumn. His worry peaked upon seeing Autumn's face, her eyes were closed and her usually cherry pink lips were dull and tinted with a light shade of blue. Taeyang coughed profusely as he pulled her further up the beach. Her body wasn't moving. Heechul's eyes widened, she looked dead and Taeyang didn't look too hot either. His friend's face deathly pale as fear caked his tired brown eyes.

Water scoured out around her as Taeyang removed her sodden shirt. Without hesitation he compressed her chest, he pushed as hard as he could without breaking her ribs. Fear tingled against the tips of his fingers as she remained unresponsive under his hands. Her skin as cold as fresh snow. He kept going, his bloodshot eyes wild with fear. Time seemed to slow down as he focused everything that he had onto her - willing her to live. He opened her mouth blowing air into her lungs before compressing her chest again. During the millionth compression her body jerked violently as water squirted out from her mouth and she coughed, choking. Taeyang acted quickly, turning her onto her side patting her back with a firm hand. She continued coughing for a couple of minutes as more water came out of her mouth before she wheezed, trying to breathe.

"It's okay Autumn, I've got you," Taeyang reassured her as he continued to pat her back.

Her coughs died down as she passed out.

Taeyang pulled up her body into his arms placing her in a protective hold. Heechul looked around as a multitude of thoughts clattered within the clogs of his drunken mind. He didn't know what to do. Taeyang's brother hadn't returned yet and they were miles away from a hospital. He clumsily paced the white sands watching Taeyang and Autumn as he did so.

Taeyang felt his chest constrict. He checked Autumn's pulse. Her heart wildly beating under his fingers as he did. He just had to do something. So, he whipped off his red sweatshirt and wrapped it around her shivering body. Autumn flinched slightly at the rough movements as she went in and out of consciousness. Her eyes hadn't opened yet. He knew that his sweatshirt was wet, but it was better than nothing. Plus, he wanted to protect her privacy.

"Come on, Autumn please open your eyes," Taeyang urged her as he stood up with her bundled in his arms.

Autumn groaned as her eyelids twitched. Her body felt numb and cold as her awareness began to flood back into her limbs. She could hear Taeyang's voice reaching out to her. In the depths of her mind, she felt his presence and wanted to see him. After struggling a bit, her eyes opened, they were a little bit bloodshot and glazed over as she tilted her head to look at him. Wisps of death laced her blue and very tired hues as she did her best to stay awake. She even tried to speak but Taeyang shook his head at her.

"Shh, it's okay, leafy. Don't say anything, just keep your eyes open okay. I've got you," he whispered as he carried her back to his brother's house.

Although he was relieved that she was alive, he felt another worry creep up on him. The possibility of hypothermia. She had been in the water for too long. The risk was definitely there, that along with the fact that she had fallen unconscious again was enough to cause Taeyang to quicken his pace towards his house. Heechul followed behind them as he tried to call Taeyang's brother again. Taeyang clambered up the stairs, removed the rest of her drenched clothes including her underwear. Under normal circumstances he would have fallen apart at the sight but for now his main focus was preventing her from developing hypothermia. He then proceeded to wrap her in every single blanket he could find, even using some of his brother's clothes in order to heat Autumn up. Heechul came into the room with hot tea in hand. Taeyang left the room briefly but reappeared with a portable electric heater.

"Taeyang?" Heechul said putting down the drinks onto the beaten up desk.

Taeyang ignored him as he plugged the heater into the socket, turned it on, and switched it to the max heat setting until it clicked. He perched himself on the bed as close as he could to Autumn's limp body without sitting on it, still ignoring Heechul as he did. His only concern right now was Autumn. Nothing else mattered.

Taeyang stayed diligently at her bedside. Heechul came in from time to time to check on the two. He tried getting a hold of Taeyang's brother, but he wasn't answering his phone. Guilt pinched at his thoughts; the only reason that Autumn was in this position was due to his recklessness. No matter what he did, his past actions always seemed to cast a shadow in his life and the people he was around. The sound of heavy pacing came from upstairs. Given the way in which Taeyang had reacted to seeing her on the edge of life and death it became very obvious to Heechul just how deeply his friend's feelings for this woman ran. He had never seen Taeyang act like that before, he looked so defeated when Autumn wasn't breathing as if a part of his own soul would die if she did not survive.

After putting on some dry clothes he waited. For hours Taeyang sat. Watching every little twitch of her face. Every moan. He waited for her to come back to him. He held her hand in his own burning the feeling of her delicate skin into his mind. He didn't know when he had started to but at some point, he began crying. He kissed her limp hand as he continued to watch her.

Autumn opened her eyes slowly feeling a little dazed. She felt awful. Her muscles ached, her head felt full, and her memory was foggy. She looked over at Taeyang whose eyes were puffy, his face a little sunken in, and his hands were currently gripping her own.

Taeyang cleared the tears from his russet eyes, his face flushed with a dark cotton candy pink as he stared at her in relief but also wonderment. Albeit her beauty remained just as captivating despite her sickly state. There was silence whilst they sat there. She coughed, startling him.

"Are you okay?" he asked Autumn as he leaned over and felt her forehead.

She nodded giving him a tiny smile. His breath hitched upon seeing her shiver.

Taeyang lay down beside her, taking her into his arms. He couldn't let her get sick. He just couldn't risk losing her again.

"Autumn, I'm sorry, I shouldn't have hit Heechul or you, I shouldn't have hidden your manuscript, and I shouldn't have yelled at you the way that I did earlier. It was wrong of me, and I hope that you can forgive me," he whispered as his eyes watered a little.

Autumn didn't say a word in response since she was still gathering her thoughts. He continued, his heart jerking with every word that rolled out from his tongue.

"I've been stupid, and immature. You got hurt because of me. What I did early was wrong. You were dead when we found you,"

Autumn's head pounded relentlessly but she got the gist of what Taeyang had said or rather confessed to her. Her skin radiated with intoxicating heat that made her feel like she was in Hawaii, his words gravitated her back to the here and now. She moistened her throat with as much spit as she could summon before speaking to him.

"L-listen, I am hurt, and angry, but more than anything I just feel betrayed, like why did you lie to me?" coughing as she did, some spit landing on the side of her mouth.

"I-I don't know. I just didn't want you to go yet. Beyond that I enjoyed reading the manuscript. I know that I should have told you the truth but I just couldn't," he explained before wiping the side of her lips with his thumb.

Autumn considered his words. She could hear the guilt dripping in every syllable. It pained her.

"I appreciate that. I just wish that you had told me sooner. As far as the other stuff goes, let's just agree that neither of us have been doing much thinking lately. Beyond that, I don't have it in my heart to hate you. I forgive you, just in future, don't lie to me, okay?" she said looking deeply into his brown eyes.

Taeyang nodded as relief washed over him, he couldn't believe what he was hearing, his mind simply wouldn't allow it. She could have perished, her manuscript would have never seen the light of day, and he was partly to blame for that. How could she be this merciful? He expected her wrath but instead she seemed almost... loving. He looked into her eyes, there was a peace that seemed to reside there despite what happened. Autumn gave him a weak smile as she noticed the curiosity in his chocolate eyes before coughing involuntarily. He let go of her hand and touched her forehead. Autumn was warm, not feverish. Still, he didn't want to take any chances so got off the bed and left the room to retrieve something.

Taeyang re-entered the room with a blue and silver can.

"W-what is that?" she asked him cautiously.

Autumn hated medicine.

Taeyang pulled back his lips forming a gentle smile. "It's a herbal tonic, it's for hangovers but it works on sickness as well," he answered before going over to the bed and cracking open the can.

It fizzed as the metal pin popped up. Taeyang helped Autumn sit up in the bed and get comfortable. He then placed it towards her mouth. She sniffed it, a strong scent of ginger hit her nose making it twitch, as the metallic edge touched the crease of her parched lips.

"It's not drugs. I promise you that this will help," he said tipping the tin towards her mouth.

He tipped it at a steady pace into her waiting mouth. She allowed it to flood her tongue, the spiciness of the herbs tickled her throat as she swallowed it. Her eyes closed, her head spinning, discomfort pounding behind her eyes. Taeyang supported her back with his free hand inwardly cringing at how pain stricken she looked as she drank. But he ensured that she drank it all.

After a little while, Autumn started to improve. She was sitting up now sipping on a cup of barley tea. Taeyang had placed an ice pack against her arm for a while before spreading a green herbal balm across it that he picked up whilst he was in Taiwan. According to the practitioner that sold it, this balm could heal any bruise or cut within twenty-fours but he hadn't had the chance to try it yet. So, he decided to test Autumn with it to see if it would help her heal faster.

Autumn smiled at him. He was being incredibly sweet and gentle. Although she was somewhat suspicious of the snot like balm, that he was putting on her since she didn't like alternative medicine or really any medicine. However, she figured that if it stopped her arm from hurting then it was worth a shot.

Heechul sat in the room not speaking, he spent a while being engrossed in the newspaper he had picked up from the kitchen table. Once Autumn was finished, he took the cup from her and left the room. Her mouth opened before closing, she wanted to ask Heechul what had come over him last night, but she didn't want to hurt him further.

The bedroom door closed as Taeyang came back in with a snack in his hand.

"You've got to eat something, leafy. Here," he insisted putting a Choco pie towards her face.

"What about you, aren't you hungry?" she asked Taeyang looking between him and the treat.

"I'll eat once I've had a nap. You need to regain your strength," he informed her nonchalantly.

She tutted her mouth before taking the chocolate biscuit into her hands and biting into it. The biscuit crunched as she enjoyed it. He smiled, before leaning back to turn the heater off. Autumn had warmed up by now and the room was starting to feel like a sauna. There was still no word from Taeyang's brother but he assumed that his sibling probably got blackout drunk at the bar since that's what he liked to do sometimes. He shook his head. "It's not my business what he does," he thought to himself before watching Autumn finish her choco pie.

A little while later...

Autumn sat on the bed waiting for someone to say something about last night. Heechul had his head down whilst Taeyang looked out of the window pensively. They had spent the last hour like this after Autumn asked Heechul why he behaved the way he did the night before. It was as if uttering a word would cause a greater rift to form between them. That is, until Taeyang cleared his throat and decided to speak.

"The handkerchief belonged to his former fiancé. He got so drunk that he mistook you for her," he stared out of the window.

Autumn mulled his words over. Sympathy curled around her heart upon hearing that. There was a plethora of questions forming within her mind over this situation but she didn't want to be too invasive. She couldn't help but wonder when he had a fiancée and what had happened to her.

Heechul was tight lipped when it came to himself and not wanting to spend forever dwelling in silence Taeyang spoke up.

"Basically Autumn, Heechul met a girl who travelled here from Japan. Her father was a big tech mogul, very affluent, and had less than noble connections. Anyway, he planned on giving his daughter away to a family friend whose son was the director of his father's bigger company. One that was just as large and just as profitable."

Autumn found herself clenching her teeth as she listened.

"She came to Korea and met Heechul during one of our after-show parties. The connection was instant. He was done for and when he looked at her you could see how much he adored and loved her." Taeyang explained, feeling awkward at the last part.

Autumn looked over at Heechul who looked a sad state as he sat there hunched over. She couldn't help but feel pity for him, his luck with women was truly ghastly.

"She loved him too from what I observed, but the threats from her father became severe. She wasn't allowed to leave her room at one point. The crazy part is that she was back in Japan when her father enforced this rule. Supposedly, the girl went on a tirade and posted a blog over it. She damaged her father's reputation by revealing that he had a mistress," Taeyang added.

Autumn gasped; her eyes comically big at this revelation but a small part of her felt joy that the girl's father received some karma.

Taeyang laughed. "Oh leafy. You're so silly," he thought breaking his pace momentarily before he went on with the story.

"The father then decided to unleash his wrath on Heechul who was kicked out of school amongst other penalties." A dark look came over Taeyang. "Anyway, after she found out about this she decided to run off, she paid a couple of her fans to help smuggle her out of Japan and get to Korea. She even went so far as to have one of them pretend to be her. That worked initially, her family and the press fell for it. This helped remove the microscope-" he paused to check that he had used the right word,

Autumn nodded before he continued,

"off them. She then met with Heechul, and he tried to convince her to go home. He didn't want her to stay with him because he was afraid of what her father would do, once he found out. He loved her but he needed to keep his kneecaps." he repressed a laugh.

"They went off to get married; they were in the middle of reciting their vows when a group of thugs busted into the venue and dragged her away from him. It's just a haze after that because he was beaten up in such a serious way," Taeyang continued, as the humour faded from his tone.

She furrowed her brow as she asked, "So what happened after that? And what happened to the girls who had conspired with her eh?"

Taeyang licked his lips as he leaned forward before continuing.

"The fans who helped her were imprisoned, and received three years each. Her father tried to get Heechul prosecuted for kidnapping. It was dicey, he had a lot of power, even people associated with Heechul were being shamed and accused of helping him commit this heinous crime. The girl in question was sent to a boarding school in China. He erased her information from everywhere. He essentially disowned her after that," Taeyang fidgeted with his ring.

Autumn made a disturbed face.

"How can someone just be erased? Is it even possible?" she challenged in her mind before voicing her opinion.

"These kinds of people have ways sadly." Taeyang somberly stated.

"That's horrible! it's not like Heechul did anything evil," Autumn exclaimed.

"I know but these people don't think like that Autumn," Taeyang responded moving away from the window to join her on the bed.

The more she thought about their respective backgrounds the more Autumn realised that none of them seemed to have had it easy in life. Her own childhood came to mind as she thought about it, the loneliness of that time always brought a twinge of pain to her. To think that they had similar experiences really saddened her.

"Do you think, she's even alive, eh?" she asked glancing over at Heechul who was sleeping deeply.

"That I'm certain of but Autumn, as you may have guessed by now, honour is very important in this country and what transpired was a really big deal. My company even came down on me for associating with him. Even now I have to be careful sometimes," Taeyang explained to her his hands twitching as he did so.

Autumn noticed this and addressed him once more.

"Tae, you weren't a thug or a hooligan for helping your friend. You did the right thing. Even, if the people around you didn't agree with it, I know that you are a good man,"

This caught Taeyang off-guard, not only her words but the look of sincerity that shimmered within the lagoons of her blue eyes. He rubbed the back of his neck, she certainly had a way with words, it was jarring how she could reach him without him needing to say too much.

"I guess you are right, thanks leafy," he praised her before looking at Heechul who was still sleeping.

"The joys of a drunken stupor," Autumn commented as she looked at Heechul.

Taeyang laughed.

"I'll give him a cup of ginseng tea once he's awake," he announced before turning his attention back to her.

"Sounds good," Autumn responded smiling between the two men.

For a while they sat there until Autumn decided to voice a thought.

"I really don't like your company Tae. They treat you like a product," Autumn admitted causing him to sigh, shaking his head.

She was starting to seriously dislike Taeyang's situation, his bosses were so harsh for reasons that were dismal most of the time. Taeyang looked at Autumn, taking in the way her nose twitched when she was pensive. He noticed that she did that a considerable amount.

"I'm just grateful that he managed to stay in Korea and was still able to get a job. Other people have had to leave for less," he said playing with his ring as he did so.

Autumn rolled her eyes.

"True but it's just stupid, Taeyang. People here take things too seriously. In Canada it wouldn't be a big deal," she remarked pouting her lip.

Autumn didn't understand, although she tried, things were totally different here. Back home, people were very forgiving, and scandals just weren't common. It made her curious as to what other scandals Taeyang has been a part of but made a mental note to ask him at a better time.

Autumn and Taeyang just sat there for a bit as Heechul slept. Autumn thought about something her agent had once told her. "You regret the things you wish had done more than the things you wish you hadn't." Her words whispered around her. Autumn had to admit that her agent was better at the life stuff than she was most of the time. She found herself missing her, and if Autumn were honest with herself, she really missed Canada. She missed the glorious conifer trees, the adorable wooden houses, the friendly and sweet attitudes that made the country so homely. Taeyang noticed the look of sadness that came over Autumn's features before it quickly vanished and was replaced by a remorseful look that made his torso constrict suddenly. She looked into his wide eyes as if she was trying to escape into the confines of his soul.

"For what it's worth, I'm sorry. I've not been the easiest person to deal with, but I do appreciate your help even if you did lie to me. I know you did it because behind that weird, hard shell of yours, you do care deeply for others," Autumn said, her voice gentle.

Taeyang nodded in acknowledgement, he didn't know what to say.

"Forget about it, we are just as bad as each other. But I'm glad that you're alive," he admitted.

Which prompted Autumn to stick her tongue out at him. Any lingering tension in the room evaporated entirely now. He repressed a yawn, but knew that he needed sleep.

"Well, I'm going to go get some sleep. Given the circumstances, I think that we should use the jet later on to return to the mainland. I want to make sure that you are okay to fly first," Taeyang said the sincerity filtered through his voice.

"Thanks, but I'm okay just sore," Autumn admitted before leaning over to hug Taeyang.

This surprised Taeyang but he returned her embrace being careful not to hurt her further.

As they pulled apart their faces were only a couple of inches away from each other. Every iota of rational thought died within Taeyang's mind. They were so close. He leaned forward; he could feel the warmth of her breath against his own, drawing him further into her gravitation, she was the universe, and he was a mere atom revolving around her. He was okay with just falling into her for the rest of his life. Her body was his sacred temple and gladly he would succumb to his knees and worship it with full abandon.

In this space, all she could see, hear, smell, feel, and touch was him. His presence consumed her in ways that no other man could. A warmth that bloomed within her gut pierced her modesty, there was no virtue when you were playing with a force as intemperate as Taeyang. His lips ghosted hers, so close to Elysium, all he had to do was push forward when the door suddenly crashed open. This made them both jump backwards. Autumn tumbled back onto the comfy bed, whilst Taeyang crashed onto the floor. Before them stood his brother, whose face transitioned from mischief to surprise. This was starting to feel like Groundhog Day for both Autumn and Taeyang.

Autumn nipped at her lip refusing to look at Taeyang's brother, her mind was frazzled and her heart was doing a marathon across her ribcage. She wanted to do nothing more than drag Taeyang back onto the bed and kiss his wonderous lips. He made her feel a variety of things - turbulent, angry, happy, giddy, depressed, it was weird but it made her feel alive. Logic didn't exist when he touched her in a way that felt divine and spiritual.

Taeyang on the other hand felt irritation as he regained his balance and walked past his brother. "Trust that brother of mine to ruin the mood." Taeyang thought to himself as went off to the bathroom to sulk. Jung-Hwa gave him a confused look but let it slide as he turned his attention to Autumn. She looked somewhat ill and from the side of his eye he caught sight of Heechul sleeping on the chair. However, his observation was broken when he saw the state of the room, his eyes went wide – it was a complete mess!

Taeyang was in the process of brushing his teeth when something in the corner caught his eye. He spat the foamy blue toothpaste into the sink before wiping his mouth off with a clean face cloth. Squinting his eyes, he noticed a black device in the corner. He plucked it from the corner carefully before inspecting it. Now that it was closer, he could make out the object clearly, his brows furrowed for a few seconds before his face darkened and his lips twisted.

"A recording device," he muttered under his breath.

He grabbed the fluffy face cloth that he had just used with his free hand then wrapped the device within it. A multitude of questions infiltrated his mind, he wondered if Chen was behind this too. The device was proof they were being spied on, but what for? why? Taeyang asked himself as he creased his eyebrows.

Dinner was filled with silence, Taeyang hadn't made a single remark but just glanced at Autumn pensively. Heechul was nursing a hangover and the bruises that now formed blue and black dots on his face, he had used various concoctions almost breaking the blender in the process to feel better. Jung-Hwa had spent the hour prior cleaning up and fixing the damaged bedroom which he still wanted answers for. Autumn offered to help clean up but was refused. She rubbed her eyes that were bloodshot. Despite a restful sleep she still felt a bit depleted but her arm was almost completely healed. The concerned looks she was receiving every time she moved a little bit or groaned from Taeyang and his brother were getting too much to handle.

Autumn put down her fork before speaking,

"I wish you both would stop looking at me like I'm going to break. Also, Jung-Hwa, as far as the room goes, Heechul and Taeyang had a fight last night. I got in the middle of it, and well I went to go clear my head when I was swept into the sea. But Taeyang can give you the other details since I was out cold during certain parts," Autumn looked expectantly at Taeyang.

Taeyang played with his meal before shoving the plate away. He didn't want to say a thing. Last night was too unpleasant, as far as he was concerned, it never happened.

"I don't remember," he grumbled before getting up to leave.

Autumn sat back in her chair folding her arms. She was growing tired of Taeyang's wishy washy attitude plus she was exhausted. She stood up clearing the plates away before dunking them into the sink and leaving. Heechul groaned, holding his head not caring for the excess noise whilst Taeyang's brother sighed. "Those two are so stubborn and ridiculous, it's painful to watch," he thought to himself.

Taeyang swiped a greenish thick hoodie from his brother's closet before getting changed. They were preparing to leave the island. He checked his phone. There were a few missed calls and obscene text messages from his manager Chen. "Just what I need today," he grumbled within his head before shooting Chen a text making up some kind of excuse about his absence. Since the whole money incident with those two men, Taeyang had a gut feeling that his manager's actions were deeper and more sinister than he initially thought. The only problem was telling Autumn and Heechul. They would want to come with him and he didn't want anyone else involved until his suspicions were confirmed. Plus, he wasn't an idiot he knew that Autumn was mad at him for his reaction earlier, but he couldn't help it. His thoughts were a flurry of troubles for him, and he didn't want to think about Autumn's lifeless body again – it was overbearingly painful.

Autumn had just finished putting on a brown, skin-tight dress and black cardigan that she had found in Jung-Hwa's closet in an old box. When Taeyang barged into the room and grabbed her wrist.

"Come on Autumn! We are running late!" Taeyang said before pulling on her uninjured arm.

This annoyed Autumn who yanked her arm away. First, he claimed to forget how she almost died this morning and now it's like he couldn't wait to get rid of her. To make matters worse, she had barely had time to read her manuscript which fortunately was undamaged.

"Look, I know that you want to get back so that I can get home but you don't have to be a jerk about it!" she snapped planting her hands firmly onto her hips.

Taeyang on the other hand said something under his breath that was inaudible to Autumn, his back stiffened before he turned to face her.

Anger and hurt brewing in his chocolate eyes.

"I'm a jerk? That's cute, Autumn. I'm a jerk for helping you, even saving your life last night," he seethed.

She pointed her finger at him,

"Ha! You little liar, you do remember what happened last night!" she accused him.

Hurt flashed in his eyes before he grabbed her finger getting into her face.

"Of course, I remember! How could I forget, you almost died you idiot!" he snapped back at her before pushing away her finger.

She hesitated at that, her anger becoming sympathy upon seeing how hurt Taeyang looked.

"I'm sorry but don't call me an idiot!" Autumn snapped back with less bite this time.

"Whatever," Taeyang responded before walking off.

It was unbeknownst to Autumn that Taeyang was really struggling with his feelings. All he wanted to do around her was hold her, protect her, and he found this desire to be in her space unnerving.

The three of them said their goodbyes to Jung-Hwa before they left with Taeyang making a mental note to pay his brother back for the damage they had done to the room.

The plane ride was suffocating. Heechul looked at Autumn who was absorbed in her manuscript. Taeyang decided to sulk in the bathroom. Autumn fought tears intermittently, taking the opportunity to read the pages of her manuscript to make sure that there were no niggly mistakes that needed fixing or any plot inconsistences with the characters and such. Everything looked great, and there was one part in particular that stuck within her throat. When the main protagonist left his family to save them from his other relatives who wanted to kill him because of who he was. She never realised how much this book

161

mirrored certain parts of her life until she gave it a proper read over. It was the best piece she had written. Every element of it screamed authentic.

Heechul bumped her ankle to get her attention.

"Uh Autumn? Are you okay?" he enquired.

Autumn didn't say anything and instead shook her head as tears dribbled down her face. He sighed before speaking again.

"Wanna talk about it?"

Autumn smiled slightly before closing her manuscript over.

"Thank you. It's hard to know what to say, if I'm honest. Taeyang doesn't express himself well. He gets close then moves away. It's really starting to hurt me," Autumn said, clutching her manuscript.

Heechul listened intently as she continued,

"I can't spend the rest of my life being lured in then kicked out, it isn't fair on me or him. I vowed that after I escaped from my toxic family that I would lead the happiest life possible. I can't be constantly mispositioned like this and be okay with it. I know that he is your friend, but this situation is hard for me." Autumn looked out the window at the clouds.

The clouds had grown monochrome and heavy yet the air was still humid.

"That's understandable. He is a good guy, just a stupid one sometimes," Heechul replied cringing slightly.

Autumn sighed before speaking again.

"I suppose you are right but that's not enough. I have a life in Canada; it might not be as glamorous as a K-pop idol's but it's my own slice of peace and I can't give it up for an uncertain future and someone who can't properly express how they feel to me,"

Unfettered pain reflected off her glassy blue irises as she stared longingly towards the sea of clouds. He rationalised the situation, if they really wanted to be together, it could work especially if his stubborn leader learned how to communicate. Korea and Canada are distant, like 5,172 miles apart distant but they could always video chat. In his mind, if they both feel this way, they should at least try.

"Would you stay if Taeyang was honest with you?" Heechul asked her.

Autumn considered the question for a couple of minutes before responding.

"If he told me the truth and made an effort to change, then I would stay. Sasaengs and backlash be dammed, I'd be lying if I said I was thrilled about the number of girls who were so fond of him but it's part of his job. I accept that,"

"He'll come around. Just have faith Autumn," he told her before patting her head and walking off leaving Autumn confused as she watched him walk down the plane's aisle.

Heechul knocked on the light wooden door of the bathroom. He opened the door and saw Taeyang sitting on the toilet playing a purple game boy.

"Taeyang, are you okay?" Heechul asked.

Taeyang shrugged his shoulders, he kept his eyes on his game turning up the volume as he did so. Heechul rolled his eyes before snatching the device from his hands. Taeyang leapt up at him, frustration evident on his good-looking face.

"You annoying son of a bitch," he snapped at his friend as tried to snatch back his device.

Heechul reversed trying not to trip up, gulping he now realized that he had pushed the right button, but the effect was stronger than he had anticipated. He was now being glowered at; it was apparent that the shreds of restraint Taeyang had been using were about to break so he switched strategies.

"Come on Taeyang, learn to take a joke," he said.

"A joke? I'm not in the mood Heechul," Taeyang said before hitting his friend's arm and grabbing back his device.

Heechul flinched as the pain zipped across his shoulder. He puffed up his chest, teeth clenching, as he squinted his eyes in an attempt to mask the pain. Which reminded him, once they were done, he needed to ask Taeyang for some karate lessons because he was really out of shape. This pause to think was ended within a minute as a hearty laugh filled the room. Taeyang found his friend's scrunched up expression amusing so much so that it made him laugh.

"You look like a shrivelled-up prune man," Taeyang remarked his anger quickly leaving him.

Heechul faked hurt by grabbing his chest but was relieved to see a glimmer of hope in his stubborn friend's attitude. They both laughed at that.

After the laughter had died down, Heechul decided to test the waters.

"So, about Autumn..." he started but was interrupted by Taeyang.

"There's nothing for me to say. She's leaving and she has her manuscript," he responded.

"I know but it's obvious that you mean a lot to her. Why not just talk to her?" Heechul asked, folding his arms.

Taeyang was unsettled at this point so he put the game boy down and continued...

"I just can't. Please don't push me on this Heechul," Taeyang fiddled with his ring.

"I'm sorry man, I didn't mean to upset you. I care about you both. Just talk to her before she leaves. You'll regret it if you don't," Heechul responded before patting his shoulder.

Taeyang sighed, he didn't like this situation. But it wasn't Heechul's fault.

"Look, it's fine, just leave me alone for a while," Taeyang said before resuming his game playing.

Heechul nodded before leaving.

Taeyang shut the door and punched it with his free hand as soon as Heechul left. This situation was killing him inside. She hadn't even left yet and he was already stressing about them being apart.

Upon entering the mainland, Taeyang left Heechul and Autumn in order to meet-up with the detective. He went in a taxi this time, his body still throbbing from last night's heroics. The meeting was taking place at the detective's office that was hidden away in a narrow alley. Taeyang sat across a well-dressed gentleman who eyed him thoughtfully for a moment before discarding his nearly finished cigarette. He pushed forward a brown paper folder. Taeyang opened it; the document had a variety of information. Pictures, notes, dates, documents, and such. Part of him wasn't surprised by the evidence presented to him yet he questioned how Chen could have done this much damage without him noticing. How did the press not notice? They were avid stalkers for any scrap of gossip that came along about Dark Star Seven. Which reminded him, he pulled out the listening device from his pocket before placing it onto the coffee-stained table. The detective raised a brow at Taeyang before retrieving the device. He was hoping that the detective could salvage an audio feed from the thing or at least get a serial number. He turned his attention back to the documents as the detective inspected the device.

On the first page were pictures of his manager. Turns out that Chen went to the adult 'room salons' which was no surprise to him. He wasn't the most virtuous man, but it was whom he met up with that caused Taeyang to gasp, the woman in the pictures was Amber. He pushed the picture closer to his face, squinting just to be sure. Her modified cheekbones were prominent, and he knew that it was her because no other woman had the kind of stare that she did. Tossing the picture down Taeyang couldn't help feel a tinge of pain at the betrayal. As far as he knew she was a successful model and actress so why was she working at a 'salon room'. There were more questions than answers at this point. He looked to the next folder, there was paperwork filed, mostly fraudulent tax documents, odd purchases, and a receipt from a DVD room.

Taeyang rolled his eyes at this; it really should not come as a surprise that Chen was fiddling with the system but what he couldn't understand was the contracts. There were former rookies' names on here, most of them never reached debut excluding a lucky few. But from what he can tell, Chen pocketed some of the money that the company was supposed to receive. "How did they not know? unless Chen forged the numbers..." he thought to himself.

After reading every piece of evidence thoroughly he managed to deduce that Chen had not only collaborated with the sasaengs in order to make money from him but also to sabotage anyone or anything that got in the way of Dark Star Seven. After all that was a big earner for Chen. Disgust laced Taeyang's drying lips; he was sick of being lied to, exploited, and treated with such little regard. He needed to see this for himself. He decided to go to the adult salon and catch Chen and Amber.

The outside of the building looked like the average karaoke club but as he stepped inside and was escorted to one of the rooms, he realised it was anything but that. The walls were grey, with pristine white leather couches against the walls with a modern TV mounted on the wall. Unopened bottles of sparkling water sat on the polished table. Two speakers, at each top corner with a bamboo plant sitting on a table in the bottom left corner. An ice bucket was stationed under the wooden table. Dumbfounded, he stepped around the table. The lighting in the room was poor, a strong smell of generic bleach laced the room also. He hid and waited.

Amber shifted on the leather couch. The feeling of an invisible gun against her head. Taeyang was taking no prisoners, once word got out, she knew that her career was finished but at least this way, she would avoid being dragged down with Chen.

"I hope she's worth it, Taeyang," she begrudgingly muttered as she waited for Chen to arrive.

She adjusted her dress trying to prevent her cleavage from spilling out. She checked her face using her portable mirror that she retrieved from her imitation designer bag. Sweat was causing her foundation to cake. She recoiled at the sight; her foundation wasn't cheap. Sighing, she closed the portable mirror and stuffed it back into her bag. She just wanted to get this charade over with.

Chen entered the room slamming the door behind him causing the frame to tremor slightly. Amber jumped back bumping her head on the wall. Rubbing that spot on her head in annoyance she took a look at the older man in front of her. She could tell that he had a couple of drinks in him before he uttered a word. He smelt like a case of expired whiskey from an abandoned brewery; although he was clean shaven which was a switch from his less than maculate condition usually.

"He must be planning something," she mentally speculated trying to not give anything away. His eyes looked between her and the tall bottle of alcohol with an expectant expression on his face. Blinking, she smiled before arranging the glasses and started pouring them a drink. Her hands trembled slightly, the pressure mounting with each second. The temperature in her body climbing to suffocating levels as she tried to balance her poker face with the fear of the impending threat of Chen's actions if he were to be displeased.

She poured him a glass. The iodine-coloured liquid trickled against its sides. Each bead like dot slinked down causing a sea of alcohol to form. His eyes became narrow and impatient as he observed the filling cup. At lightning speed, he swooped his hand down and snatched it from her hand before swallowing it up. The bottle in her hands slipped as fear started to get the best of her. He wiped off his mouth before belching loudly.

It hit the ground but didn't smash, the liquid had done the damage already. The carpet had a prominent stain on it. Her forehead creased as she did her best to dab it until a grunt snapped her from the boring, and soul crushing task.

"Just another thing to pay for," she grumbled to herself wishing a dragon would swoop down and eat her where she was kneeled.

The carpet stabbed against her skin; she didn't want to think about the other stains that had come to pass on this carpet.

"We have a deal, Amber. If you can't fulfil it, I'm sure that there are other willing females that won't... protest...like this," he stated, the malevolent streak never leaving his voice.

He yanked her wrist, twisting it hard until it clicked. She winced but refused to show weakness in front of this brute. Chen leaned in closer. His eyes dull, and lifeless, the stale brown in them made her feel as if he was consuming her whole soul. Greed oozed from him like gunge coming out of a weeping pimple.

The crustiness of his large hand made her want to scream out to anyone that could hear. His presence was violating, he truly embodied the essence of a twisted, cruel, and empty shell of a human being. He released her now bruised wrist as he gave her a twisted grin.

"Stop it Chen, I've fulfilled my part...a few times now. Besides that, you are the one who needs to get rid of Autumn not me," she stated coldly

He grunted before lowering his voice to speak.

"I will, but don't forget, you are under my orders, understand?" he leered over her.

Amber held her wrist, shrinking back, a dirty look directed at him as he smirked, she was many things but a whore was not one of them. Money had been tighter, and jobs had been less as of late. Her pretence in front of the others that her life was a glamorous fairy-tale, was just that, pretence.

Taeyang recorded the entire interaction resisting the urge to wipe that ever-growing smirk off Chen's face. Amber became progressively unhinged the further into the conversation they went. Both of them discussing how to dispose of Autumn with Chen doing most of the conspiring. Chen didn't take notice of Amber's upset, as he downed a glass of sparkling champagne. Once his manager had left, Taeyang came out from behind the couch, a scowl planted firmly on his face. His heart stalled seeing her in such a drunken and upset state, a part of him wanting to reach out and hold her but the anger and betrayal he felt at what they were conspiring to do to Autumn killed that feeling dead. Amber didn't notice him she was too wrapped up in self-pity.

"She made her bed," he said vehemently in his head as he heard sobs echo from behind him.

He left the building without looking back.

Chapter Ten

Chen's Deadly Endeavour

Autumn had been working on the first draft of her next novel when a loud thud nearly sent her flying from her wooden chair. She flexed her fists as she sat in Heechul's house. The boys had been over and Soon Woo had stayed back so that himself and Autumn could catch up.

"If Soon Woo is playing a prank on me, I swear to-" she was cut off but another noise that made her flinch. That's when she recalled their last conversation,

"So, Soon Woo, do you have any plans tonight?" she asked as he was fiddling with his hair.

"No, sorry, but tonight I am visiting my aunt. Since, we have a little free time, I'm going to catch up with my family," he told her before licking his hand and slicking it across the strands of his dark matter coloured hair.

He extracted himself from the couch tossing his pocket mirror in her direction. She shook her head laughing her keister off at his antics as she caught the mirror with her hand.

End of Flashback...

Autumn's mind kicked into high gear as she heard a noise in the house, if it was the sasaengs then at least she was ready this time. Thinking on her feet, she tucked her draft down the back of the TV. She heard a heavy thudding sound become insistent. Searching around she did her best to find any object that she could fashion into a weapon but there was only a solitary fan. She held it to her body before creeping beside the living room door.

A pair of grubby manly hands thrusted themselves onto her shoulders, her shrill scream caught within her vocal cords as adrenaline, anger, and surprise hit her all at once. The fan tumbled from her grasp. She pushed herself forward not caring about what happens next just as long as there was distance between herself and the intruder. She elbowed his stomach with inhuman strength causing her assailant to stumble backwards. Her eyes became a comical size when she saw who had attacked her.

"C-chen?" she stammered moving back with a sense of terror yet surprise.

"Why is he here?" she let slip from her mouth causing him to chuckle before prowling into her space.

He didn't voice a response but the way his hands were flexing and the sweat drenching his brow told her all she needed to know. He was here to harm her.

Chen snickered; his brows wild, his eyes bulging, bloodshot and resembled a demonic wild beast not a gluttonous mortal man who smoked like a coal fire and ate anything that was salty, greasy.

"Chen, please just think about this-" Autumn was cut off mid-sentence.

Chen smacked her across the face knocking her off balance as he pulled something out of his pocket, her cheek burned in a thousand splints of fire. He was on her in an instant, she elbowed him with the sharpest part of her bone before stamping down on his foot pushing him back. She didn't see the object in his hand, her eyes were too watery from the pain emanating from her face to notice it. Chen grabbed her hair before stabbing a liquid filled syringe into her neck.

Autumn's eyes blurred and the world spun as her mouth opened.

"Taeyang, please...save.." she wheezed before collapsing onto the floor.

Taeyang could feel a sharp and very painful sensation darting across his heart from the second that he stepped inside. The intensity of it was of such magnitude that he fell onto his knees and spluttered out as the fiery feeling attacked him brutally. He blinked back tears, never in his life had he experienced this searing level of agony. He searched his mind for answers, but the pain was poisoning his thoughts making it hard to think with any rationality. Taking a deep breath, he allowed himself to get back together before going further. The silent buzz in the air made him feel as if he were being watched.

Looking around, his eye caught a paper corner. He crouched pulling on it carefully. He managed to release it from its spot behind the TV and his eyes widened. It was a draft,

"Autumn..." he murmured as he read the page.

He placed it onto the table. He wasn't sure why she had chosen the TV when there was the couch but it's quite possible that she was in a tight jam. Then a mark caught his eye. On the floor, a pool of dark crimson blood congealed, his heart constricted. There was a fifty-fifty chance that it was Chens's blood but if that were the case then wouldn't she still be here?

Taeyang had no clue as to where Chen could have gone but he didn't care. When he saw him, he knew that he was going to kill that bastard for what he had done. Taeyang bolted out of the building and pulled out his phone to get help, Hyeon picked up.

"Hey, what's going on?" Hyeon asked.

"That bastard Chen has abducted Autumn," Taeyang informed him.

"What? Why?" Hyeon asked in complete disbelief.

"It's complicated. Look, I have an idea where he might have taken her. Call the police and let the company know. Thanks, Hyeon," Taeyang said before hanging up.

As Taeyang continued to run, his phone rang, an unknown number blaring at him. He answered it with haste, his nerves shot to pieces and his heart hammered. A deep, gritty, and yet scratchy voice that was dipped in contempt cut through the short-lived silence. He heard feminine screams in the background. He tightened his hold on the phone, his gums bleeding with the level of pressure he was applying against his mouth as vexation corroded his heart.

"What did you do?" Taeyang snapped.

"Nothing....yet," Chen responded.

"If you do anything to her Chen, your downfall will be merciless and by the time I'm through with you, there won't even be fingerprints left to retrieve," he warned before hanging up, cutting off Chens's sadistic laughter.

Chen had a sharp throwing star pressed against Autumn's neck as she struggled within his vice grip. Taeyang arrived at a disused warehouse in heart of Seoul's red-light district. He growled at the sight before him, the murderous tint in his eyes escalating into erratic twitches of his hands. The veins in his neck popped out beneath the skin as his jaw became clenched tight. He ground his teeth before stepping forward.

Chen scoffed. "Pretty here, good for business,"

Taeyang despised the implication but knew that if he fell for the bait then Chen would win, and he couldn't allow it. His pride, his heart, and to be frank, his sanity was on the line right now.

"What is this about, Chen?" Taeyang asked darting his eyes between Chen and Autumn.

He struggled not to go ballistic and kill Chen right there and then without a second thought. He had manipulated him, conspired against him, and exploited him along with the other members but none of that compared to the line he had crossed the minute he put that blade to Autumn's neck. A foreign emotion flashed in his eyes. One which she had never seen in their previous interactions.

"Give me the documents you got from that detective and a million Korean Won. Or she dies." Chen spat.

"No, because even if I had them on me you are so cowardly; you'd probably kill her just to be sadistic." Taeyang retorted narrowing his eyes.

"She'll die, Taeyang. If you don't. You wouldn't let her die now, would you?" Chen taunted him.

Memories of his mother filled his mind. He'd seen the pictures of his mother's dead body after she had been found. The coroner ruled it a suicide, it was a grotesque sight. One that was etched within the hollows of his haunted soul. Images of Autumn's bleeding, unmoving body made him heave, there was no way in hell he was going to let the same fate befall her. His father had failed their family, he would not allow himself to do the same. This made him vow, that from now on, no matter what happened, he'd always be there to save her.

Chen's eyes were feral yet dull. Taeyang moved forward. He had to do something, but if he moved a toe out of place then Chen would flay her like a mullet in a fishery. That image itself was enough to put him off seafood for life. She did her best to put a little distance between herself and the steel point whilst he was distracted. She looked to Taeyang, with her eyes she tried to gesture over to the rope at the metal support against the concrete wall. He was giving Chen a death glare that made her shrink back into herself.

The two were at a stalemate. Autumn had another idea. This situation was starting to feel like deja vu but she used all of her energy to uppercut Chen's chin causing him to drop the throwing star. She tumbled across the ground as Taeyang charged at Chen. Winded, she lay there, her ears ringing. Blurred images of the two men passed her line of sight. Her heart slowed as her breathing became shallow and clumsy. Shadows crept around her as her body shutdown and her eyes closed.

Chen tried kicking Taeyang, but his reflexes were on a hypercharge, so Taeyang turned before kicking the man in the groin. Chen let out a gut churning wail before charging at him. He heard a crack as the bone shattered under the power of his strike. Chen's eyes popped in his sockets; he resembled a strung-out hobo who was riding a dragon into the pits of a chalk village. He didn't use these kinds of moves very often. But when he did, a bloodbath was guaranteed. Chen started coughing, his lungs wheezing as ugly black mucus prickled his mouth.

Taeyang glanced at Autumn's unconscious body making sure that she was still breathing but Chen was crafty. The air was knocked out from Taeyang's lungs as he fell forward. Chen had managed to obtain a discarded hammer.

"Not so tough now, are we?" Chen taunted him.

"Bad move." Taeyang seethed before jumping and kicking Chen across the face.

The hammer fell from the portly man's hand as he stumbled back. His mouth bleeding.

Chen had caught him off-guard with that attack. For a man who was an old glutton he could move as fast as a younger man. However, he was still older. After trying to charge at him again Chen was taken down by Taeyang as he delivered a final blow to his face. Knocking out his yellowing front teeth. His body dropped hard and fast onto the concrete as blood pooled around his mouth and now his head. He grinned at that before rushing over to Autumn.

Taeyang pulled her body into his arms. He kissed her forehead as he cradled her gently. He took this as an opportunity to check her over. He checked her arms. Face and neck. He narrowed his eyes upon seeing a scratch on her skin. "At least the blade didn't break her skin or catch an artery," he thought to himself just feeling grateful that the throwing star didn't actually pierce her neck.

Autumn opened her blue eyes. Looking down at her was a tired Taeyang. His lips pulled back gently as she looked up into his hazel eyes. Her mind pulled together the pieces of what had happened. She had been working on the draft of another novel. She heard a loud noise. Chen attacked her. Then Taeyang came. She hit Chen then everything went black. Slowly she sat up trying to compose herself. A wave of emotions flowing through her veins exploding into various thoughts and questions.

Taeyang watched her feeling relief that she was okay but guilty since she had been attacked and kidnapped for the millionth time this week. He wondered what was going through her mind. She had gone through so much in such a small amount of time. And if he were honest so had he. Chen had betrayed him and as much as he didn't like the man, he had to admit that on some level it did hurt.

As Taeyang became lost in his thoughts, Autumn grappled with her own. Here she was, alive, but she had come too close this time. Using her fingers she traced the pink line across her neck that stung as she touched it. Chen had almost killed her. If Taeyang hadn't been as smart as he was or he hadn't known his manager as well as he did then she would have died. This couldn't happen again.

Autumn realised as the two sat there in complete silence that she needed to leave South Korea. Before she actually died.

"I can't be here anymore," she whispered, this revelation weighing her down like a magnet dangling from the neck of a peacock butterfly.

Her words went unheard by Taeyang who picked at the drying blood on his knuckles.

Autumn didn't cry this time which made him feel uncomfortable. She wasn't saying anything either which only added to the already suffocating tension between the two. She just sat there staring at her knees as if she was drugged or stunned. He didn't know where to begin. So much had occurred. This was just the latest ordeal that they had to cope with.

The world became smaller as they waited for the police to arrive. At some point Taeyang had put his arms around Autumn. He didn't know what to think. Chen had manipulated him. Part of him felt cut into two. His dream was to be the top dog of his profession and known all over the world but if the price of that was exploitation and becoming a lifeless drone slaving under his greedy overlords who cared little for his wellbeing, then he wasn't sure if this path was right anymore.

Taeyang was brought out of this state when Autumn pushed herself out of his embrace without a word and stood up with her back turned to him.

"I'm tired Taeyang, I can't keep doing this," Autumn spoke as pain laced her voice.

"What do you mean? Do you think this is easy for me?" Taeyang retorted as he also stood up.

"N-no but this is too much! Between stalkers, thugs, and everything else I'm completely drained! This just isn't worth it especially when I know that you are just going to pull away from me again!" she exclaimed as tears began quivering in her blue orbs.

"Autumn what do you expect from me? Whenever I get closer to you something bad happens. Do you really think I want to keep seeing you hurt? I'm not good with this emotional stuff. You should know that by now!" Taeyang yelled, turning her arm to face him.

"I get that! But it doesn't change the fact that I can't stay here! Because there is a good chance that there is nothing for me to stay here for, if I'm being honest with myself," Autumn said her voice cracking as she did.

"Nothing? Now who's the immature one, running away from their responsibilities? After all isn't that what you said to me before. If after today, you still think that I don't care about you, then go home. I'm tired of having to save you. I'm tired of feeling confused. I'm just tired of this shit, leafy!" Taeyang shouted as his anger rose.

Taeyang felt deeply hurt by her words. So, he was nothing now? He just didn't understand where Autumn's mind was at this point. Yes, she had gone through a lot but he had managed to save her. Did his efforts count for nothing in her eyes? He did his best to keep his flaming anger under control. She was the most confusing woman ever.

"I'm tired too! And if that's how you feel then fine! I'm just trying to be honest with you Taeyang!" Autumn snapped, clenching her fists.

"Don't echo my words back at me! You're not being honest here; you are running away! But you know what? Go, if that's what you want to do so badly!" Taeyang retorted, glaring at her.

"Fine!" Autumn shouted.

"Fine!" Taeyang yelled at her.

They glared at each other as tears formed in their eyes.

Taeyang was done. He had no more energy left to give her. He felt so defeated. He felt destroyed by this whole situation. And by her.

"Goodbye, Taeyang." Autumn cried before she ran off.

Taeyang stood there with tears pouring from in his brown eyes as he watched her leave.

The police arrived along with his bandmates.

"Goodbye...my leafy," Taeyang whispered before wiping his eyes.

The authorities were thorough in their interrogation. Taeyang pulled on his hair several times as he sat across from an investigator who had the personality of a dead fish whose throat had been lacerated by a feral cat. Chen was taken to the hospital, and according to the conversation he had overheard two officers having, he was in the ICU. Well, this caused a small smile to grace Taeyang's face.

"Good, that bastard deserved what was coming to him," he remarked as he sipped on a cup of tar like coffee.

The detective ignored him as he signed the papers in front of him before getting up and joining a colleague in the hallway.

As it turns out, his now former manager had accumulated a lot of charges in the past but had changed his identity numerous times and moved from different parts of the country. His real name was, Hachem Wong, a former business teacher who was fired for improper actions toward female teachers. He was also an accessory to a petrol station theft in Busan in his younger days. He was looking at a severe fine on top of the hefty sentence he was going to receive for tricking the tax man. He was going away forever. This gave Taeyang a great deal of pleasure as he finished what was the worst coffee he had ever drunk.

Chapter Eleven

Words To Be Said, Before She Left

Taeyang returned to his dorm. His body burned from the strain of his dance practice as his thoughts simmered. Consumed by Autumn. Everything reminded him of her. A song he would hear in passing. When a woman walked by wearing a floral garment. It made his heart flinch and his bones vibrate. Even the break and pay increase that his CEO, Mr Quay had given him and the others as an apology for Chen's actions hadn't helped lift his spirits. It was also going to be the season Autumn soon. That was going to be torturous. He looked around trying to find a distraction.

He eyed a packet of new cigarettes that were on the desk. Temptation kissed along the contours of his neck up into his ear.

"Do it Taeyang, it's right there," a voice in his head uttered sinfully.

He smirked before shoving the pack onto the floor and proceeded to stomp on it.

"The day I get so stressed and beneath my perfect self that I resort to smoking, is the day that I finally shave my head and run off into the woods," he said, a swagger in his tone.

Still, this arrogance only lasted for a couple of minutes before Autumn came drifting back to his mind. He kicked a swivel chair from its place under the desk across the room causing it to hit the wall and as a result chip the paint. "She's gone. I can't change that," he thought to himself angrily.

At the airport, Autumn sat with her suitcase waiting for her flight to be announced. Her agent although she was royally perturbed at Autumn had agreed to meet her once she was back in Canada. Her life was about to be normal again, yet a deep sadness filled the cavity of her heart. The last few days had been the most entertaining she had ever experienced aside from almost dying multiple times and being kidnapped. But the worst part of leaving was that Taeyang wouldn't be there. Regardless of their differences she really had fallen for him. Now, he wouldn't speak to her, and knowing how busy his life was he probably never would again. Tears crept into her ocean eyes before sliding down her cheeks as she clutched her luggage close to her heart.

Taeyang punched the bed before flinching. He was losing his mind, his last argument with Autumn constantly nipping at him. His feelings confused him significantly, on one hand he wanted to kiss her to the point of deflowering her body but at the same time he wanted to toss her into the nearest volcano. It was difficult, as much as he wanted to blame her, he knew that he couldn't place complete blame on her. After all, he was the one who took her luggage and hid it from her, his part to play in this mess was blatant. He pulled at his blue hair, he should go to the airport and stop her but if he was caught up in anymore scandals his career and the career of his bandmates would be over. He rambled to himself, letting out his destructive rage upon the furniture until the door opened. Hyeon popped into the room along with the rest of the band. Taeyang paused, grasped the lamp he was about to smash before blinking at them. Hyeon stepped forward, gently pulling the lamp from Taeyang's hands. He placed it onto the floor. Internally cringing at how messed up their room was but also feeling a pang of sadness that Taeyang felt like this was the best way of dealing with his emotions.

"The guys and I have been talking and we think that you should go after Autumn," he said whilst smiling sympathetically.

Taeyang felt the last vestige of rage dissipate before confusion filled him.

"Hyeon, if I go after her, Dark Star Seven will be toast. You know that, right?" Taeyang said to him.

Hyeon smiled. "We know but Taeyang, you've sacrificed everything for us. It's time for us to return the favour," Hyeon stated warmly.

"There are plenty of other countries that we can perform in and we have a solid fanbase so we'll be fine either way. We have each other and the music, that's all we need man," he spoke, as the others nodded in agreement.

Taeyang turned his head to the side as his throat started closing up and his face started to grow a dark crimson. Hyeon, and the others grinned, with Soon Woo snickering before speaking.

"Ooooh, it looks like oppa has feelings,"

This earned him a deathly glare from Taeyang.

He just grinned causing Taeyang to jump over and hit Soon Woo over the head with his hand before he chased him. Taemin interjected by throwing a partially beaten pillow at Taeyang who easily deflected it before throwing a plushie back at him.

Taeyang put Taemin into a headlock before messing up his permed hair. Taemin protested as a fit of giggles came out of his mouth before Hyeon muscled himself in-between the two and broke them up.

"Break it up boys! Taeyang has a girlfriend to save," he slipped in, earning a playful glare from the older boy.

Taeyang let go of Taemin before rummaging around looking for his phone. Hyeon thrusted it into his hand. Taemin yanked a random hoodie out from their closet putting it over Taeyang's head as Soon Woo thrusted a wallet into his jean pocket. He adjusted the hoodie and arranged himself to look smarter.

"Her flight leaves in half an hour, good luck leader," Hyeon said giving him a thumbs up.

"I found this Taeyang, at my place. I think it's for you," a voice interjected.

Heechul entered the room. It was Autumn's handwriting. He hesitated for a moment before opening it:

"*Dear Taeyang,*

I didn't know what to say before. If I'm honest, my mind has been a chaotic whirly mess ever since I stepped foot in this country. Then I met you and all of the things I thought I knew stopped making sense to me. You are the most stubborn, flippant, and confusing man that I've ever met and yet, I can't bring myself to hate you. When we fight, it never stung me as much as seeing you with Amber did and realising that there's someone who is better for you. Someone who isn't, nor will ever be, me. So, this is me, letting you go. I want a million different things for you but most of all I want you to be happy. So, be happy Tae, life's too short. I love you.

Yours truly,

Autumn Willows"

His heart tumbled at her words. She loved him.

"Autumn..." he said to himself, blinking as he reread each line.

Taeyang touched the edges of the thin paper as if he was holding gold dust in his hands. His throat tightened. The day Amber had come over, she acted weird, like completely out of character. Then when he went into the room, he caught sight of her shuffling paper away from view. It must have been the letter. He bit back nausea as he recalled their fight. It had been nasty, and now he understood why she had been so defensive with him. There were so many things, a trillion apologies, he needed to make to her. He needed her in every way a person could need another person – it was maddening. Taeyang could see her pain from their last argument. Her departing figure haunted him. He knew that if he did not tell her how he felt then he would regret it for the rest of his life.

Taeyang hadn't thought this through as he dashed away from the dorm with the letter stuffed into his other jean pocket. There was no plan. No direction. Just feeling. Just her. So, when he ran into the middle of the road to stop a taxi heading his way, he wasn't surprised that the taxi driver gave him a bewildered look, and a few choice words that would put most sailors to shame. Taeyang badgered the taxi driver to hurry up as they drove, her flight was set to depart in twenty-five minutes. His nerves and desperation fuelled his next set of actions. He pushed forward, kicked the driver out of the moving car before closing the door and putting his foot down on the accelerator. He took shortcuts through alleys, almost running over a group of aghast elderly people in the process. Taeyang raced through a vegetable stall causing varieties of pak choi, cabbages, and piles green onions to go flying all over the place. His phone started vibrating like crazy.

"The CEOs are going to have a stroke when they see this," he thought aloud before speeding through a busy marketplace causing chaos in his wake.

Clothes, confectionary, trinkets, and such went flying into the air as he put his foot down on the pedal. Screams and shouts echoes all around as other cars swerved to avoid him. His phone started to ring obnoxiously. Taeyang couldn't see the caller ID through the constant notifications he was receiving and let it go to voicemail; nothing was going to stop him from getting to his leafy.

Autumn dried her eyes with a scratchy tissue, before stuffing it into her coat pocket. Her gut nagged at her to stay, but she just couldn't. Her responsibilities had been neglected for long enough, she couldn't afford to be selfish, her fans were excited for this book, so it was her obligation to get it out to them. She retrieved her phone from her pocket and swiped up on Taeyang's contact. The line rang, she bit her lip to the point where the skin split just a smidge. She stood up from her seat as the phone rang. It continued to ring until his voicemail answered her. She stomped her foot. Tears threatened to spill from her blue eyes once more as she roughly hung up before stuffing her phone into her dress pocket. She never got the chance to tell him how she had felt. Autumn had been incredibly upset and now it was too late.

She picked up her suitcase and started walking to the terminal. Her heart sank further with every step, her hands felt numb, the emotion draining from her very being. Intrusive thoughts started pecking at her mind, the carcass of her optimism flickering like a candle in an empty church. Yet her heart still grappled with the thought that he would magically come to his senses and sweep her off her feet into the burnt orange sunset. However, that was mere fanciful thinking, Taeyang was a human being, and a notably stubborn one at that. She had to accept this fact.

Taeyang ditched the car as soon as he made it to the airport. He shoved past people causing one older woman to throw her walking stick at him along with a string of curses. He didn't care, all he wanted was Autumn. There were waves of unfamiliar gawking faces which only mounted to Taeyang's waning patience and increasing desperation. He darted around the airport ignoring the people who gasped at him as they recognised him. He didn't have time for that either. His mind was racing, paranoia set in. Taeyang knew that he was in hot water with everyone now, but his thoughts were consumed with Autumn, with righting his wrongs. He checked his phone as sweat trickled down his brow and he could have died in the spot on which he stood. He had a missed call from her, he frantically sent her a text as he ran around trying to find her.

Taeyang eventually spotted Autumn, who looked crestfallen to say the least. He sprinted towards her, pushing his legs as far as he could. Defying his protesting ankle. Knocking over random people, luggage, and a couple of plastic chairs but nothing was there, in his mind only she existed. He managed to reach her just as she was at the terminal door.

"AUTUMN!!" Taeyang shouted causing her to turn around.

Was this a delusion caused by the sting of unrequited love and a lack of sleep? She was brought out of her thoughts by the sensation of a firm hand on her arm. Taeyang pulled her arm and used his other hand to snatch her suitcase, a little harder than he meant to, causing her to wince.

"I-I'm," he puffed out trying to catch his breath.

She looked at him sceptically.

Taeyang grabbed her again but less aggressively this time.

"A-autumn I-I'm so sorry," he said trying to control his intense emotions.

She paused looking at him cautiously but said nothing as he confessed,

"I've put you through so much because I couldn't express how I felt before. You make me so angry; you make me feel so worried, you contradict me, you're stubborn, and you have the worst taste in perfumes like, calm it, with the god-awful lavender woman. But, when you aren't with me, I feel so incredibly hollow, I need you more than I have ever needed anyone. Before you came here, I wanted to be the biggest Korean Idol in the world without really knowing why. It's only when you left, I discovered that I wanted to be successful so badly because I had nothing of worth inside of me. You gave me my soul back, leafy. I love you and I want to be with you. I don't care about what anyone else thinks. If it stands in the way of us being together then it goes and that goes for my career too," tears pouring down his cheeks, as he stared into her eyes that were now gushing like a waterfall also.

"Oh Taeyang. I had no idea...I thought that you didn't care. But I love you too, I love you so much, and whatever happens I will always stay by your side, you, beautiful jerk," she said grinning as her voice cracked.

He put the suitcase down and grasped onto her face with his hands gently before his lips descended against hers as they cried together.

All of the emotions she had been holding onto now merging with his own as their souls connected. They were one. Finally, they were whole.

She pulled back, her teary ocean eyes widened in realisation,

"Where's my-?" she didn't get a chance to finish before Taeyang held up her suitcase.

"You mean this?" he said playfully through tears, causing her to gently clip him over the head before she consumed his lips with her own once more.

Autumn allowed herself to fall completely into Taeyang's unconditional love, not caring about how crazy she looked or where they went from here or even the book's deadline. She now had her manuscript and her man, and in the end, that's all she ever needed.